# THE HUNTED

# THE HUNTED

## A Novel

## KATHRYN PTACEK

Walker and Company
New York

First published in the United States of America in 1993
by Walker Publishing Company, Inc.

Published simultaneously in Canada by Thomas Allen & Son
Canada, Limited, Markham, Ontario

Library of Congress Cataloging-in-Publication Data
Ptacek, Kathryn.
The hunted : a novel / Kathryn Ptacek.
    p.  cm.
ISBN 0-8027-1227-4
I. Title.
PS3566.T33H86   1993
813'.54—dc20     92-21669
                  CIP

Printed in the United States of America

2  4  6  8  10  9  7  5  3  1

*For*
*Emily and her Dudley*

*Out of the dead, cold ashes,*
*Life again.*

—John Bannister Tabb

# Hunters Heights, New Jersey, 1975

## <u>SATURDAY</u>

# ONE

"Blow out the candles, sweetie," Astrid Fields said in her breathy voice with the syrupy Southern accent. "Go ahead and be a big girl now."

Jessie Mae Morrison, who was turning eleven on this sixth day of September, pressed her lips together and tried not to frown. Her mother meant well; it was just that Jessie hated being called "sweetie." She hated being treated like a five-year-old.

"C'mon, Jess," Patrick said. Her stepfather's tone was slightly impatient. "People are waiting."

*Waiting for you*, is what he meant, she knew. Waiting for you to screw up. Waiting for you to fall on your face.

She glanced at him, then at the faces ringing the dining-room table. It was her mom and Patrick, and some kids and a handful of adults her mother had wrangled into coming to this party. The Fields and Jessie had just moved into their new home in Hunters Heights, New Jersey, and Jessie hadn't been there long enough to meet new friends. However, that hadn't stopped her mother. Astrid had set out yesterday afternoon and walked up and down the block, going to each house, introducing herself, explaining the situation ("my daughter is having her birthday and we just moved in, so she hasn't made any friends"), inviting kids not even her age to Jessie's party.

A handful had come, no doubt tempted by the prospect of free cake and ice cream and all the sodas they could guzzle. Hey, who wouldn't give up two hours of her afternoon for food. Jessie would have gone, had she been invited.

There were the usual helium-filled balloons—all shades of pink because her mother was convinced Jessie just loved that color, when she really *hated* it—and pink and white streamers, and big gold letters strung together, which read "Happy Birthday." There had been stupid games, which her mother had organized, and some music, and her mother had insisted that she dance with the boy down the street. Pete, she thought he'd said his name was.

One of the boys, maybe seven or so, she guessed, stuck his tongue out at her. She ignored him. A girl a year older than Jessie snapped her smelly grape gum and looked bored.

Politely Jessie blew out the candles, and everyone politely applauded. While her mother was cutting the cake and Patrick served the chocolate-chip-mint ice cream, which her mother knew she didn't like either, Jessie made good her escape and sneaked out onto the front porch.

Hunters Heights.

She wrinkled her nose. What a dumb name, she told herself, as she sat, arms wrapped around her legs.

And worse, she was in *New Jersey*! She had heard all the stories about it. Dumber yet.

She could hear the adults talking and the kids laughing and there was some music—the Bee Gees—and wrinkled her nose further at that. So far, they were all too involved to notice she was gone.

Good.

She glanced up and down the street, lined with its imposing maple and oak trees. They were old and tall, and made a thick emerald canopy over the street with their arching branches. Canopy. She'd learned that word last year and thought it was pretty neat.

A climbing rose bloomed alongside the steps, and she could smell the perfume of the flame-colored flowers, and hear the droning of the bees as they darted from one blossom to the next. She wasn't afraid of bees or wasps or spiders like a lot of girls she knew, and that made her feel good. Only *babies* were scared of bugs.

The sun was warm on her face and legs, and for the first time in many months she almost felt—content. But she didn't want to feel that. She wanted to be angry and unhappy.

She jammed her hands into the pockets of her yellow shorts. The pockets were filled with the peanuts that she'd planned on tossing to the squirrels, and now she glared at a gray squirrel bounding across the lawn. It scampered up a tree, vaulted to a branch, raced along one of the telephone wires, then zipped down the trunk of another tree. She almost smiled, but caught herself just in time.

[ 4 ]

It being Saturday, Jessie had lots to watch. A boy about three in orange shorts was darting back and forth across his lawn, his arms thrust straight out from his body like the wings of an airplane. Behind him loped a golden retriever. A pregnant woman pushing a stroller had just rounded the corner and was heading up the street on the other side; she paused to talk to some skinny guy washing his sports car. Jessie could see that next door another woman, maybe her mother's age or a bit younger, was on her knees doing something to a garden where there were lots of pretty blue and pink and white flowers. A black dog crouched nearby in the grass, panting.

Some old gray-haired guy in checked shorts and a white T-shirt was out mowing his lawn. He'd stop ever so often and wipe his glistening face on his T-shirt.

Jessie wrinkled her nose again. How disgusting.

"Jessie!" someone called.

She ignored the summons.

It was a pretty neighborhood, she admitted reluctantly, with houses at least a century old, wood, and two stories high. Most were painted white, while the woman next door had a pink one with maroon and white trim. Patrick had snickered when he'd seen it, but her mother had said she thought the unusual color was beautiful and at least the house was painted authentically as opposed to theirs, which was simply plain ol' white with boring green shutters.

Dumb, dumb, dumb.

She sighed.

Here it was already Saturday, and on Monday Jessie would be going to her new school. It was probably dumb, too. She'd missed all of this week, and she'd have to hurry to catch up, and the kids probably wouldn't like her; they'd tease her about her name and the way she spoke and she'd come home humiliated, shamed, unable to go back to school.

She wished.

All the other kids would know the rules—she wouldn't, and that would be the worst thing of all. Not knowing. And no one would tell her. The other kids would just wait until she made a mistake, then they'd laugh.

Her mother didn't understand; her mother said everyone had to go through the same things when they were young. Mom was wrong, Jessie knew. No one had ever had to go through the terrible things she was going through. No one.

She wanted to go home so bad. She had told her mother that,

too, when they arrived at this place, but her mother had simply said that this was home now.

"Dumb-ass home," she said softly, then sneaked a glance around to see if anyone had overheard.

Jessie didn't really have to worry; *they* were inside. Some of the adults were laughing in that too-loud tone grown-ups got when they were drinking, and she just bet that Patrick had brought out some beer or something. He always had a "little beer" before dinner, and after.

Dad didn't drink beer.

She put her head down on her knees and swallowed quickly. She wouldn't cry. Not now. Not outside where someone could see. Where *he* might see. *He* had called her a baby once for crying; she hadn't forgotten that. She was going to make sure he never saw it again. Never. Ever. Again.

It was hard not to cry when she thought about her father, and she could feel the wetness in her eyes, feel it dripping down onto her knees. She missed him so much. She wished she'd gone with him to the store that time, and then she'd be dead, along with him, and not living in this awful house in this awful town with this awful man.

She heard the rumble of Patrick's voice and squeezed her eyes shut.

To give him credit, he really wasn't terrible. At least she kept telling herself that. He didn't beat her or anything like that. She had heard what some of the other girls in her old school had said about their stepfathers, and at least Patrick never touched her like that either. Just let him try, she thought fiercely, and she'd kick him right in the balls. Usually he just patted her on the head, or the shoulder. She could cope with that. So far.

He wanted to be her friend. That's what he'd said when he'd started to date her mom, and then after the second time he had said for her to call him Patrick, and he would call her Jessie, even though she hadn't asked him. For months she hadn't referred to him by name; just "you." She just couldn't.

Then her mom had gone and married the jerk. And her dad wasn't even dead a year.

It wasn't right.

Patrick still wanted to be her friend. At least he hadn't wanted her to call him "Dad." She couldn't do that, because he wasn't her father, after all.

Stepfathers didn't count.

The tears kept coming, and she was feeling slightly dizzy now. She breathed slowly through her mouth, tried to count to a hundred—that's what her dad had always told her long ago to do if she was upset or angry or sick—and she couldn't even get past sixteen before the funny feeling hit again.

She was sick to her stomach, but she couldn't do anything about it, because she seemed to be floating in a grayness. Or rather she wasn't floating. She just *was*. Wherever she was was cold, very cold, too wintry for early September in Hunters Heights, New Jersey. There was a great empty aching inside her, as if she were hungry for food and for something else. And all around she could hear horrible voices calling, crying, screaming. Voices of women and men, and children her own age. And there was a smell, a terrible stench, and her stomach rumbled, and she was going to lose her lunch, and—

Jessie jerked her head up and gasped.

The stink went away.

A slight headache remained, a throbbing behind one eye, and she blinked rapidly, hoping it would go away almost immediately like all the others had done. She stared at the placid street in front of her. She could still hear the old guy's lawn mower, and the squirrel had come down off the tree and was cautiously approaching her. The retriever barked at a bird. She waited for a few minutes, but the sickness didn't return, and gradually the headache went away, just as she knew it would.

She'd had these . . . spells . . . ever since moving to Hunters Heights. She called them spells because that was what Grandmother Morrison said all the Morrison women were prone to. One week when Jessie was only seven she had spent the summer with her father's mother down at the woman's farm, and she had learned that the Morrison women were sensitive, and they—those spells—always came on when a girl was close to becoming a woman.

Or at least that's what Grandmother Morrison had declared. But she had died when Jessie was only eight, so she never got a chance to ask her all that she wanted to. Her mother didn't much like her mother-in-law and had kept claiming the old woman was filling the child's head with nonsense. Jessie's father had just ruffled Jessie's hair, then winked solemnly at her.

It wasn't nonsense, Jessie knew. It wasn't. Her grandmother said the Morrisons had been in America a long time and *knew* things. What those things were, though, she took to the grave with her.

[ 7 ]

Jessie had not yet said a word to her mother about these spells, because her mom would get worried, then increasingly frantic, and either put her to bed right away and make her drink room-temperature ginger ale, which she just hated more than anything, probably even brussels sprouts, or she'd take her right to the doctor and he'd give her a shot and some gross-tasting medicine, and she still wouldn't feel any better. Or maybe her mother would think she should see a psychiatrist. She had a friend in her last school who'd been to the shrink and it wasn't much fun, her friend said. Her friend said she had started making up things to say to the guy because the sessions were so boring.

Jessie knew, though, that shrinks could put you in mental hospitals where people peed their pants and wandered around like one of those zombies she had read about.

She didn't want that. Best, then, to keep these things to herself.

The spell today had been the worst so far. She thought it was because it was her birthday, and she was nervous.

Jessie sighed. The woman next door glanced up. She must have heard Jessie. Jessie looked away.

She took out a peanut and held it out with a steady hand to the squirrel sitting a few yards away. Its bushy tail twitching, it chittered and crept closer. It was within inches of her hand when the front door opened and the squirrel darted off.

Jessie did not turn around, but she could imagine her mother standing in the doorway, a frown on her face, her hands planted on her hips.

She noticed that the woman next door was watching them.

"Jessica Mae, how many times have I told you not to let those squirrels get near you? Those creatures have all sorts of diseases and are filthy to boot, not to mention havin' ugly bugs as well, and they just might bite you, and you'd have to go to the hospital."

To the stupid Hunters Heights Hospital. Why did her mother always have to use her full name? Frankly Jessica Mae was an ugly-bug name.

"Jessica Mae?"

Jessie said nothing. Her mom was scared of everything sometimes. She was afraid that Jessie would fall and cut herself and get lockjaw. She was afraid that Jessie would catch some disease called meningitis which she said schoolchildren sometimes caught or maybe pneumonia or something equally awful. Her mom was afraid all the time, and sometimes Jessie thought she was being suffocated by her mother's love. They didn't even have a pet because her mother

[ 8 ]

thought the pet would breathe on Jessie and give her a dreadful disease or bite her or scratch her or leave hairs on her clothes that would somehow prove fatal—suffocation, maybe? Her dad had wanted her to have a cat and a dog, maybe even a horse, which her mother absolutely forbade because horses could bite with those big ol' teeth and they could buck and were most certainly unpredictable animals, and, why, consider the statistics for little girls falling off horses and promptly breaking their necks. No sir, no horse for Jessica Mae, said her mother firmly.

"Jessica Mae, did you hear me?"

"Yeah."

A foot tapped. "How many times have I told you that it is 'yes, ma'am,' not 'yeah'?"

"Hundreds," Jessie muttered under her breath, her hand closing around the peanut.

"What's that?" her mother asked.

"Nothin', ma'am."

"Don't you think you should be inside with your *guests* rather than out here mopin'? This is not the way a proper hostess behaves, young lady."

They're not my guests, she wanted to say, but she didn't.

"Aw, come back in, Astrid," Patrick called. "Let the kid be. She probably just wanted a breather. It's all the excitement, you know." He belched, and a woman inside tittered.

Excitement. Right, Jessie thought.

Jessie heard the screen door slam shut as her mother went inside. At least she'd escaped another lecture.

Jessie hated it, though, when Patrick defended her, because then she couldn't hate him as much and she really wanted to hate him with all her heart for taking her father's place. Only sometimes the hate just wasn't there.

The woman next door got up and brushed the dirt off the knees of her jeans. The black cocker spaniel wagged its tail eagerly. The woman waved to Jessie.

Jessie hesitated, then she lifted her hand. She watched the woman go inside.

Jessie glanced back at the street. The boy had left with his golden retriever, and the mother with the stroller was gone now.

She opened her other hand. The peanut's shell was cracked a bit. The squirrel wouldn't mind. She drew her arm back and threw the peanut as hard and as far as she could and hoped she hit something.

# TWO

Wendy Wallace stood by her front window and watched as her young new neighbor threw a peanut into the yard, then stood and dusted the seat of her yellow shorts. The girl stomped into the house, slamming the screen door and getting a shrill complaint from her mother in response.

Somehow Wendy didn't think that was a happy household. There was something—off—in the mother's tone; and the girl had been crying earlier. Wendy had tried not to notice, but it was hard to ignore.

She gazed outside—Phil would have called it spying—a few minutes longer, until one of the cats, the gray shorthair, rubbed against her ankles. He meowed softly, almost a kitten's sound. Behind him she heard the rumble of the small black cat.

"I know. Time for an early dinner."

The two cats and the cocker spaniel trotted after her into the kitchen. She opened a can of wet food for the cats and another for the dog, dumped the contents into their respective dishes, and watched as her pets devoured their meals.

She snagged a cookie, fetched a glass of soda, and, afternoon break over, headed upstairs.

An hour later Wendy stretched lazily, then leaned back in her small wing chair and looked out at her backyard.

Momentarily she glanced back at the next white page she had carefully rolled into her IBM Selectric typewriter and the centered words "Chapter Eighteen," which had given her pause, since she didn't know *what* was going to happen in Chapter Eighteen.

She shook her head, then looked back out the window where things were much more fascinating: blue jays, cardinals, and sparrows splashed in the ceramic birdbath set in the middle of the lawn, squirrels chased each other around the trunks of trees, and she could hear kids yelling and splashing in the above-ground pool several houses down. There were hours of light left, and she wanted nothing more than to go outside in the back and sit in the chaise and continue reading the new mystery by John D. MacDonald.

However, she had to finish her own chapter by dinner—it was her self-imposed deadline—and here it was already four-thirty.

Good luck, she told herself wryly. 4:32 already. Tick, tick, tick.

Of course, she wouldn't get any work done by daydreaming. Somehow that was more engrossing than staring at the white paper, which within the hour had taken on the appearance of a vacuum into which she feared she'd been sucked.

From where her desk sat, catty-corner to the window, she could see all of her backyard as well as that of her new neighbors. They had been moving in for the past few days, and Wendy had watched with great concentration, finding it necessary to head downstairs frequently to look out the front windows.

She had long ago accepted the fact that she was just plain nosy.

Great trait in a reporter and a novelist, she told herself firmly.

Which happened to be the only two jobs she had ever held. She'd obtained her degree in journalism from Columbia, then gone on to work at the local paper, the *Hunters Heights Herald-Journal*, for seven long years, rising from lowly obit writer to chief investigative reporter and the "star" features editor at the end ("rat race, rat race, rat race" sang the refrain in her head), and then she'd sold the book she been working on at night, thumbed her nose at her astonished boss and quit.

Just like that.

She didn't make tons of money—the best-selling authors did well enough in that department—but she did all right. It didn't hurt that she already had a house—paid off, because her parents, who died a decade before, had willed it to her.

So here she was—just snooping a little. It was, she kept telling herself, one of her most charming attributes.

Besides, what else was there to do in Hunters Heights? A tiny town in the northern section of Morris County, itself in northern Jersey, it was on the northern and western fringes of what people kindly referred to as suburban New Jersey. Not quite a bedroom community, although many of the inhabitants did commute an hour-plus each morning into New York City.

But Hunters Heights had existed long before New York City had grown into the metropolis it was now. The town predated the Revolution by several decades. A site for Colonial mining, it lay compactly on a small bluff that rose alongside an old coaching road, and had once been one of the last stops before New York. The woods, all oak and maple and birch, had been thick and dark in those days, and for two hundred years many of the wealthy had made the journey out to hunt pheasant and quail. Richly appointed cabins became the headquarters for the well-to-do in the country, and many of these bungalows still existed, although most had long ago evolved into year-round houses.

The woods had thinned somewhat since the turn of the twentieth century, particularly with the development of the past decade, but the area still retained its rural flavor. The woods clustered thickly outside town, and traces of the old forests could be seen in the strands that wove their way behind houses and businesses; the mines were all closed now, abandoned some time after World War I. Hunters Heights had a couple of banks, restaurants, pharmacies, churches, retail shops, and all the other livelihoods associated with everyday life.

In recent years the single movie theater and adjacent bowling alley had closed down, and the Dairy Queen was boarded up, so for nighttime entertainment you had to go into New York City or head off to one of the other towns nestled cheek-by-jowl to the east, in the overcrowded northeastern section of the state. Or you could drive to Passaic County, where the malls sprouted liked cement-and-glass mushrooms.

Like most of the state, Hunters Heights was not in good financial shape. Wendy didn't think it would ever become a ghost town, but it certainly wasn't the prosperous place it had been several decades before.

Mostly now it catered to the antiques business. A newly opened bed-and-breakfast inn had been ballyhooed in the local paper, which she thought looked more like a commercial shopper than a newspaper these days. The town boasted more than half a dozen "old-tyme" businesses. Tourists from the rest of the state and from New York City flocked to the place on weekends and in the summer for "bargains." With all the bicentennial hysteria, now the town practically shrieked "1776" from every business window, even though the nation's two hundredth anniversary was still a year away. You couldn't walk two feet without seeing so much red, white, and blue your eyes crossed.

Of course, how many times did a country celebrate its bicentennial?

Still, it appeared as if Hunters Heights had jumped on the bicentennial bandwagon to help it back on its feet. She hoped something good came of it.

And in the meantime, she told herself, watching things from her windows was much cheaper than the few other options open to her, not to mention saving time. It would take hours just to hop in the car and drive someplace, hang around, then drive back. This way, she assured herself, she'd get more work done.

Right. She had hours to go before she could call it quits for the night.

She took a sip of her soda, glanced at the paper, flexed her fingers, and, with a sigh, began typing.

# THREE

Dr. Emerson Thorne glanced up at his wall clock and was astonished to see that it was nearly five twenty. He had come into the office just before nine this morning to do some paperwork before he began to see patients in the afternoon. He had always made it a point of scheduling appointments for one weeknight and for Saturday afternoon. There were too many working people who couldn't take time off from their jobs during the week to bring their children to the doctor. Thorne couldn't very well have them not bringing the children in at all.

Unlike many of his associates, he preferred to practice preventive medicine. He really did hope he wouldn't see his young patients again, or at least not very often—better that he should treat them while they had simple colds than see them when they had pneumonia and his job was all the harder.

Now he smiled reassuringly at the child in front of him. The boy, not more than eleven and pale with big brown eyes, appeared very nervous. He coughed, his slight shoulders hunching with the effort. He was trying hard not to worry, but wasn't having much success.

"Will I have to have a shot, Dr. Thorne?" he asked, his voice quavering. He gasped for air and another fit of coughing racked him. Thorne rubbed the boy's back, trying to get him to relax. Frank was a very handsome child, much better looking than you would have thought after seeing his parents, Thorne reflected.

"Yes, Frank. I'm afraid so. You have a pretty bad case of bronchitis, and the shot is the best way for the medicine to get started. You'll just have to have the one today, though, and after that, you'll be taking the liquid medicine."

Involuntarily Frank made a face, and Dr. Thorne nodded sympathetically. "I know how you feel. It's the orange syrup this time, though, not the grape."

Frank looked somewhat mollified at that news. He glanced at his mother, a large dark woman dressed in a dark dress and black sweater who had sat silently through Thorne's examination of her son; in fact, she hadn't said a word since she and the boy had entered the office.

Thorne didn't mind the quiet ones. Sometimes the mothers thought they knew more than he did and would tell him what he was missing and what he ought to be doing. He disliked mothers— and fathers—like that. He didn't mind a question or two, but to have everything he did second-guessed, as if he were incapable after thirty-six years of practicing medicine— He shook his head.

"Do you have any questions, Mrs. Colangelo?"

She looked at Frank, then shook her head.

Thorne prepared the syringe, and rubbed Frank's upper arm with an alcohol-saturated cotton ball.

"Is this going to hurt?" the boy asked, eyeing the needle.

Thorne nodded solemnly. "I won't lie to you. It *will* hurt, but only for a moment or two." Quickly he stuck the needle in, the boy flinched, and it was over.

"Good boy." Thorne ruffled the boy's hair. "See. Not so bad, was it?"

Frank Colangelo shook his head and looked slightly surprised.

Thorne stuck a Band-Aid on the shot site, then sat at his desk to write out a prescription. He handed the form to Mrs. Colangelo, who just stared at it.

Frank had put his shirt back on and now took the prescription from his mother.

"She doesn't understand much English," he said with an off-handed shrug. He tucked his shirttails in and stuck the paper in his pocket.

Thorne looked at Mrs. Colangelo, so quiet all this time—and now he knew why. She probably only had understood she had to bring her son in to see a doctor, nothing more. He came around to the front of the desk and sat on one corner. He leaned toward her, and began speaking in a low tone in Italian.

She almost smiled and for a moment Thorne saw the young woman she must have been long ago. A rapid-fire exchange of Italian went back and forth for several minutes. Frank looked out a window.

"*Grazie! Grazie!*" Mrs. Colangelo seized Thorne's hand and

pressed it against her enormous breast. Gently he removed it. He shook her hand, and she tried once more to press it against her breast. Once more he extricated his hand.

"I've explained to your mother what you have and how the medicine will help you, Frank. She says she'll make sure you take every dose. Remember it won't do you any good if you don't finish it."

Frank nodded. "Thank you, doctor."

He waved to them as Frank pulled his mother from the room. He glanced at his desk calendar, set just to the right of his blotter.

The sixth today, first Saturday of the month. Next Saturday was the thirteenth, and that night his son Raymond would be home and they would be going to the Morris County Country Club, just about this hour. What an evening that would be. After all these years, to be finally acknowledged, finally rewarded.

He shook his head. It was fine to daydream, but until then he had quite a lot to do.

A few moments later the receptionist buzzed him that another patient was waiting, and Thorne strolled into the second examination room to see what ailed this young person.

As he headed back to his office a few minutes after six, Thorne made a mental note to remind Mrs. Peterson, his nurse, to check through the files of the children whose fathers were construction workers. In the past few weeks he had noticed that a fair number of them were already in a bronchial state, the way Frank Colangelo had been, and he wanted to check that. Plus he planned on going to the nursing home tomorrow morning; he had promised one of his young patients he would visit the child's grandmother.

He dropped into his swivel chair and looked outside into the twilight. Summer was gone already. The days weren't quite as long or as warm as a few weeks ago, the flowers no longer blooming as heartily . . . it was the living season turning into the dying season.

How quickly summer had come, too, this year, and suddenly it was almost over, almost autumn. Soon it would be winter.

Thorne shivered. He hated the snow and the cold and the ice and chilly winds, and wondered why he had settled this far north.

He should have set up practice in Florida like so many of his friends. It was warm year-round—never mind that in the summer it was downright sweltering; but then everything there was heavily air-conditioned—and the roads, a friend had once written to him, were practically paved with wealthy patients willing to pay outrageously high medical bills. To prove it the man had sent along over a dozen photos of the twenty-eight-room mansion he'd purchased in the Bahamas and the white Bentley he'd presented to his wife on their thirty-fifth anniversary.

But there was more to a medical practice than making so much money you had to lie awake at night thinking of ways either to spend it or protect it from the IRS.

Medicine had always been more than mere money to Thorne. If he'd wanted money, he wouldn't have gone into pediatrics. He would have studied cosmetic surgery and headed out to Hollywood, to do face-lifts and tummy tucks and this new breast implant for the stars.

His stomach growled as he hung up his white coat. Time for dinner. He drove to the diner just down the road and ordered a simple meal of two tuna melts and a chocolate soda. The waitresses knew him well, and knew not to chatter at him when he came in with his head down; it was a sign he was thinking, and didn't want to socialize. Tonight he didn't want a meal—simply food. He still had work left at the office, which he returned to at five to seven and stood at a window to look out into the last light of the day. He had sent his staff home hours ago, and his fellow doctors in the clinic always teased him about missing his golf games. Of course, he left such things to them. He had never been interested in golf or similar diversions.

For Thorne, the study and practice of medicine had always been his life. From as far back as he could remember, he had always wanted to be a doctor. Most boys his age had wanted to grow up and become firemen or policemen or even movie cowboys, but for Emerson Thorne the supreme profession had always been medicine. Luckily his parents had been able to afford to send him to an excellent medical school; even if they hadn't, he would have worked to put himself through university. He would have done it somehow.

He flipped on the lamp on his desk and sat.

He pulled the stack of folders toward him, took out a legal pad, uncapped the twenty-four-karat gold pen Dorothy had given him long ago, and began writing.

# FOUR

With great relief, Patrick and Astrid Fields collapsed into separate easy chairs in the living room as the last of the birthday guests and their well-liquored mothers and fathers filed out around seven.

Patrick closed his eyes. In the distance he heard a lawn mower. That was a reassuring noise, although it wasn't as homey a sound as the old push mowers had made. Showing your age, he thought wryly, and then looked around the front room where some of the furniture was still jumbled along one papered wall.

The professional movers had unloaded everything late Thursday morning, and the three of them had spent all of yesterday unpacking, hauling things upstairs, and switching things around. He and Astrid had been lugging boxes upstairs all day, arranging furniture, until just about an hour before the first of the guests arrived. He hadn't thought a birthday party was the best of ideas today—after all, they'd just arrived in town, they didn't know anyone, and they were hassled enough without the added strain of getting a kid's party together—but Astrid had insisted. She had said Jessie—excuse me—Jessica Mae needed a party to feel welcome in her new home. Frankly, he thought Astrid had needed the party far more than Jessie had. No doubt the girl would have been happier just going out to dinner with them. But Astrid had wanted the party, and so they'd had the party, and now they were exhausted, and they'd lost hours of unpacking time to this damned silly birthday celebration.

There wasn't much time left, either. On Monday he would go back to work, Jessie would start school, and Astrid would put the finishing touches on the house—the paintings hung on the walls, curtains at the windows, the books settled in the bookcases, the knickknacks grouped here and there, all the objects that made a house a real home.

He took out a handkerchief, wiped it across his face, and felt the sweat come away. He tucked the handkerchief into his back pocket.

God, he was tired. He didn't know entertaining kids was such a hard job. He suspected he'd rather be lugging trunks and heavy boxes around than having to smile all afternoon at a bunch of bored kids who were there just for the food and drinks.

All right, so it wasn't all afternoon; it was only four hours, but God knew, it felt like all afternoon. He knew the party hadn't gone the way Astrid had planned it; nothing involving Jessie ever went the way it was supposed to. Astrid had been disappointed by the puny turnout, but he'd thought it was a hell of a crowd considering the short time she'd had to invite everyone. So what if the kids just stood around and ate and stared at one another? He'd gotten along well enough with the adults, especially two women from down the block, both blonds, who lived next door to each other. Sisters who had married brothers.

Patrick glanced over at Astrid. Her eyes were closed and her head rested on the back of the chair. There was a slight line between her brows.

"You don't have a headache, do you, honey?" he asked.

"No, no, nothin' like that."

Astrid was prone to headaches, severe ones that, if they weren't migraines, were kissing cousins. Each time an episode came on he insisted that she see a doctor, but she kept swearing there wasn't anything that a doctor could do, and besides, aspirin and some rest would help just fine, thank you. Patrick wasn't convinced. It just didn't sound right to him. The worst part was that anything could trigger the headaches: the volume up too high on the television, the phone ringing once too often, Jessie's voice, an unexpected bill, a disagreement with him. Sometimes Patrick suspected Astrid's headaches were more psychological than physical. That didn't mean they hurt any less.

"You want a drink, hon?" he asked.

For a moment he thought she was asleep, then she stirred.

"Not right now. I just want to sit here and not move. I just want to pretend that my face doesn't hurt from all that smilin'." Her voice had a Southern accent to it—most of the time soft, but when she was angry or trying to make an impression, it grew more pronounced.

"Boy, don't I know that feeling." He grinned and then heaved himself to his feet. In the kitchen he grabbed a can of beer from the refrigerator. He was almost out again—he'd been pretty liberal with the stuff this afternoon. On his way back to the living room, he glanced out the screen door and saw Jessie sitting on the front steps again. She had come back to her party, politely unwrapped the presents he and Astrid had bought for her, eaten her cake, and talked with a couple of the kids. She had even stood at the door and said good-bye as each kid and parent left.

The perfect little hostess. His lips curled.

Then, when the last person had gone, Jessie had turned and looked at them—as if it, whatever *it* was, was all their fault—and she had stomped out onto the porch again. She just sat there, doing nothing.

He shook his head. He didn't understand only children, how they occupied themselves when they didn't have brothers or sisters to play with. He'd had three sisters and four brothers, and there'd been little enough time for any of them to go sit outside alone and sulk about some imagined slight. There had always been someone for him to wrestle with or chase or be chased by. Hell, if he had his way Jessie wouldn't be an only child for long.

He remembered earlier when Astrid had seen the squirrel; she had started freaking out. He shook his head. He was going to have to make her understand that she had to ease up on the kid. All kids like to feed animals. And well, if she did get bitten, they'd just take her to the hospital. You couldn't protect kids from everything in life. Not if you wanted them to grow up normally. Hell, a dog had chewed him up when he was nine and he'd survived it, just like he'd survived a broken leg, four cracked ribs, a sprained foot, some blackened eyes and loosened teeth, and a fractured wrist in his high-school years. All kids got hurt now and then, and there wasn't a damned thing you could do to prevent it. Astrid couldn't keep Jessie wrapped up in cotton wool for the rest of her life. It just didn't work like that. Not with kids.

As he sat again he placed the cold side of the aluminum can against his forehead. God, that felt good. It was damned hot for September; he thought it would be cooler by now. Felt like the summer more than autumn.

He lifted the can to his lips, took a swig, then belched loudly.

"Patrick." Astrid looked shocked.

"Sorry." She was a good woman, and he loved her, but sometimes she could be a prig. Well, he'd just have to loosen her up. These Southern ladies—just too prissy, for all their iron wills.

Astrid glanced up a few minutes later when Jessie wandered inside. For a moment the girl looked like any other awkward eleven-year-old he'd ever seen. Then she edged quietly across the room to stand alongside her mother's chair. As if she wanted to get as far away from him as she could.

It bothered him that she wouldn't come stand by him. He knew it shouldn't irritate him, but it did. For God's sake, he'd been married to her mother for nearly a year now. How long was it going to take her to accept him? He'd done everything he could think of, but Jessie hardly spoke to him. At least when she did, though, she was unfailingly polite. Her Southern upbringing, no doubt.

Astrid fanned herself with a magazine, lifted the front of her blouse away from her chest, and blew on her exposed skin.

"See anything interesting?" he asked. He took another drink of the beer.

"I always see something interestin' there," she said with a wink.

He chuckled.

Jessie stepped closer to her mother's chair, as if she were protecting Astrid somehow.

He was finished with his beer. "Hey, honey, want to go get me another one?" he asked Jessie.

She stared at him.

"Jessica Mae," her mother said sharply.

"Relax, Astrid."

Astrid frowned at him; her lips were pressed together. Oh God, he'd pissed her off again. It was too hot for them to get mad at each other.

The girl slipped into the kitchen and returned in a moment with another can. She handed it to him, and he noticed how careful she was not to touch him. He wondered what she would do if he reached out and grabbed her hand. He flexed his fingers, then dropped his hand into his lap. Now was not the time to start that kind of nonsense.

She went back to stand by her mother. She hadn't said a word since entering the room. Her expression hadn't changed, either. It wasn't quite somber, but close enough. At least she wasn't sullen.

Astrid's eyes closed again as she fanned herself.

"What about dinner?" she asked after a moment.

"Dunno. What about it?"

[ 21 ]

"What do you want?"

"What do you want to make?"

Astrid opened an eye. "Patrick, I swear that you are deliberately being difficult."

"That's right."

Astrid gave an exasperated sigh.

"How about we go out for dinner?" he suggested. "It *is* Jess's birthday."

"Oh, I don't want to get all dressed up. It's too hot for that. I thought New Jersey was cool in September. This is as hot as it was in Lexington, maybe even hotter. Just as humid, to tell the truth."

"Usually, it's not this blistering, believe me—it'll get cold enough pretty soon. And you don't have to get all gussied up, hon. When I was out yesterday I saw a couple of restaurants within a few miles that looked fairly decent. There's bound to be one that isn't too dressy. You know, something family-style or whatever. Maybe even a diner nearby. We could let Jess decide for us." He smiled at Jessie, who stared back.

For a moment Astrid said nothing, then she roused herself. "Okay. Fine with me. Whatever you or Jessica Mae want. In fact, I don't think I could cook anything tonight, because I don't know where all the kitchen things are yet. *You* packed those boxes, and I just can't find anything. All we have left are some paper plates."

"Well, we can't go out looking—and smelling—like a pack of stevedores. Gotta get cleaned up before they toss us out of town. Jess, you're first. Go take your shower, hon," Patrick said.

Jessie hesitated, looked sideways at her mother, then shook her head vigorously.

"What do you mean, no?" Usually Jessie was fairly obedient. He hadn't expected this.

Jessie remained silent.

"Jessica Mae," her mother said sharply. "Answer your father."

"Stepfather," she muttered.

"What?"

"Nothin'. Ma'am."

But Patrick had heard. His face hardened. "I want you to go take a shower now. You've been outside and it's hot, and you're all sweaty, Jess. You need to clean up. We all do. We smell like farmhands." He winked at his wife.

"I know."

"Well, then?"

"No."

He looked at her mother, as if to say, well, she's *your* daughter. Of course, he had said when they married that her daughter would be his as well. He meant it. As far as he was concerned, there was no ghost of Rick Morrison between them. As soon as possible, he would adopt Jessie, even though she had said she wanted to keep her father's name. Well, he was her father now. She had to learn to obey.

"Jessie." He said her name calmly. "Go upstairs and take a shower. You're holding us all up. I've got things to do. So does your mother."

"No."

He glanced at her. The girl's face was set, a slightly mulish twist to her lips. She had never thrown tantrums before, and this, while hardly qualifying as one, astonished him. Her mother acted surprised, too.

"Come on, Jess."

Jessie frowned. She wished he wouldn't call her that. It was her father's nickname for her; he didn't have any right to it.

"No, I can't."

"Can't?" her mother asked. "Or won't?"

Jessie knew they didn't understand. She couldn't take a shower. Just the thought of that tonight made her skin prickle, made her feel weird inside. She couldn't find the words to explain. She knew somehow the shower would hurt her.

"I can't. It'll hurt me."

"You've taken a shower before, honey."

"Not since we moved here."

Her mother looked astounded. "Then how have you been washin' yourself?"

She shrugged. "I ran water in the sink and used a washcloth."

Astrid's lips thinned. "This is ridiculous. Now you really do need a shower, Jessica Mae. You cannot get clean that way."

"No," Jessie said simply.

"Well, that's enough of this nonsense." Patrick stood and grabbed the girl by the hand, jerked her away from her mother before either could protest. Jessie's hand felt so small and soft inside his. How easily he could tighten his grip—

"What are you doing, Patrick?" Astrid asked. Her accent was thicker than it had been just moments before, and she was sitting up, clutching the arms of the chair with her hands.

[ 23 ]

"Come upstairs with me."

Astrid followed.

He pushed Jessie into the bathroom off the master bedroom. The room was large, but for some reason a tub hadn't been installed there. That was one of the first things they planned to rectify once they fully settled in. In the meantime, they had a shower stall, with a frosted-glass door that closed rather than slid open. The stall was spacious, and Astrid had joked when she first saw it that you could probably stash a football team in there and still have room left over.

Patrick jerked the frosted door open, shoved the shower head to one side, and turned on the faucets.

"Patrick."

He didn't answer.

After a few seconds he thrust his hand under the water, adjusted the taps minutely.

He looked at his wife. "Get undressed."

"What?"

He started unbuttoning his shirt. "I said to get undressed. We're going to take a shower. Jessie is going to take a shower with us. We're going to show her that taking a shower doesn't 'hurt.' That all you do is get in and scrub yourself, rinse, and get clean. That's all there is to it. Period."

"Patrick, I don't think this is such a good thing to do," Astrid said, her tone nervous. "I mean, she's eleven, after all, and hasn't bathed with me or her father since she was a really small child."

He glared at her. "For Christ's sake, Astrid, I'm not going to molest her. You don't have to worry about that." He glanced at the girl, who stood stiffly on the fuzzy pink bath mat. She hadn't moved since they'd all trooped into the bathroom, and she was staring down at her feet. "Get going, Jessie."

Awkwardly the girl pushed off her sandals, then inched down her yellow shorts with the flamingos sewn on the hip and pulled up her matching sleeveless top, taking as much time as she could. She touched the ring on the chain around her neck; it was her father's class ring. She had taken it from his drawer after the funeral. Her mother didn't like it; Patrick teased her about it. "Going steady?" he'd asked her a couple of times. "Daddy's little girl," he'd said another time. She lifted the chain over her head and tucked the necklace into the pocket of her shorts. Her fingers hesitated when she reached the elastic band of her cotton panties. She swallowed heavily.

Her mother finished undressing, picked up her clothes, and set them carefully on the white wicker hamper. She was in her mid-thirties, and though not a particularly active person, she carried just enough extra weight to take away the sharp angles of hipbones and ribs. The blond hair at the juncture of her thighs was several shades darker than the hair on her head. Her breasts were large, fairly firm, although she'd always joked that you couldn't be big and firm at the same time. Her skin was pale.

Patrick kicked his clothes out of the way. He had a slight potbelly, but he knew it wasn't bad for his age and for the kind of work he did, which was all indoors, all sedentary, not like when he'd worked on a road crew every summer during college. His penis was flaccid, dark pink like a limp coral snake. His chest was extremely hairy, as were his legs, and the elastic tops of his white socks had left red marks on his calves.

"Jessie."

She slowly pushed her panties down, stepped out of the rolled-up underwear.

She shivered slightly, though it wasn't cold. Far from it; the temperature all day had hovered in the eighties. She crossed her arms in front of her chest, aware that her breasts were beginning to grow, and she was very self-conscious. No one in her family had seen her naked for years. And certainly *he* hadn't. She rubbed her upper arms, tried to make the goose bumps go away.

She didn't want to do this.

It wasn't a good idea.

She wanted to go home, wanted to get away from this. She wanted her father with her. He would never have let this happen.

Her mother and stepfather were in the shower now—she could hear them moving around.

She didn't want to look. She didn't. Didn't.

But she had to.

Silently Patrick held out a hand to her, and she looked at the nude figures in the tiled shower, clouds of steam billowing up around them. She saw them, saw their naked flesh, saw—

Jessie began screaming.

# SUNDAY

# FIVE

A car horn blared, and Wendy jerked her attention back to the street.

Too late she saw she was about to collide with a car coming out of the supermarket parking lot. She stamped on the brake, felt the Rabbit shimmy, and the small car stopped. But not in time.

She felt the car shudder as it thumped into the second one. She waited to hear the breaking of glass, but she was spared that. She sighed and stepped out. At least it wasn't a Cadillac or Mercedes she'd hit; it looked like some older-model Buick. Something big and tanklike in comparison to her tiny import. Wendy didn't care to recognize most cars. Something Phil had always nattered at her about. She pushed thoughts of her ex-husband from her mind, and studied the Buick. She could see the dent in the car's dark blue door where her Rabbit's front end had slammed into it.

"What the hell do you think you are doing, lady?" demanded the driver as he got out on the passenger side. He spoke with a mild European accent, and he had long dark hair that kept falling into his eyes. He kept shaking his head to toss it aside.

Brother, Wendy thought.

"Have you been drinking or do you always drive like this?"

Wendy knew it was her fault—she'd been daydreaming—but she didn't need to have her face rubbed it.

"Look, it's just a minor accident. It's not like your precious car was totaled or anything."

"But," he gestured wildly, "it will have to be fixed now."

"If it's any comfort," she said, her voice rising, "my headlight is broken and my grille is bent. A lot worse than that little ding in your side."

"What a peculiar sense of 'comfort' you Americans have."

One part of her, much more detached, observed that she did not usually stand on the corner of Main and Nelson and argue with foreigners about their cars' wounds. One part of her also pointed out that she should have been paying attention. As if she didn't know that already.

The police arrived, and the cop listened patiently to each party. Then without breaking rhythm in his gum snapping, he told them to exchange insurance information and issued Wendy a ticket for careless driving.

By the time the two cars had been moved into the parking lot so that the rubberneckers could get by and not back up traffic any more than it already was, the cop had hopped into his car and sped off.

No doubt to rendezvous with a chocolate-frosted doughnut at the Donut Den, Wendy thought sourly. In her notebook she scribbled some information down, ripped the page out, and handed it to the man. He scanned what she'd written, as if doubting every word.

In turn, he jotted down a few lines on the back of a business card. "Stefan Marek," the flowing script read, with an address in Prague.

Czech then. She'd pegged him for a Russian, no doubt a KGB spy. Right. In Hunters Heights.

"Any relation to the Marek who runs the glassworks here?" The Marek glassworks on the edge of town was one of the more prosperous businesses left. Everyone needed glassware, which is what kept the place rolling along year after year, dip in the economy or no; not even the energy crisis had truly affected it.

"I'm his nephew," he replied stiffly.

"Um," she replied, not knowing what else to say.

Now that they had both settled down, she could take a better look at him beyond that damned lock of dark hair which had irritated her. At least he didn't wear the long sideburns that were currently fashionable—a point in his favor, she decided. He looked to be in his forties. His eyes were nearly black, and his face lean, with a few lines about his eyes and his mouth. He did not look like the type to smile often.

He was well dressed, which went against everything she'd ever heard about Communist men—weren't they supposed to have bad taste in business suits? Maybe she was thinking of the Soviets again. Marek could have passed for any business type on Wall Street. He was only a few inches taller than she, slightly stocky, and Wendy had the feeling that he was like a wire cranked too tight. One more twist, and he'd spring loose.

"Look, Mr. Marek, I really am sorry about your car. I don't usually drive this offhandedly, and I most certainly do not make it a point of driving into the sides of cars owned by visitors to our shores."

He shrugged. "Actually, it's a rental car."

"Oh good. That makes it ever so much better. I should have slammed into it then."

"Miss Wallace, please, sarcasm doesn't become you at all."

"Well, I guess the boys at the paper lied—they said it was the thing they liked about me best."

She moved toward her car. "Well, I've really got to go. Good-bye then." What else could she say? Glad to meet you? Not quite.

He inclined his head toward her. "Until next time, Miss Wallace."

"Not on your life, brother," she muttered to herself, then hoped he hadn't overheard.

She decided to leave the car where it was, since it was already in the supermarket's parking lot, and just take a hike across the blacktop. As she entered through the glass doors she glanced back and saw Marek sitting in his car, watching her. She shrugged and went on with her shopping, and with the crowded aisles and squalling children, she completely forgot about him.

When she came out of the store half an hour later, she saw that the Czech had left.

She paused at one of the outside newspaper machines to pick up the Sunday edition of the *Hunters Heights Herald-Journal*.

The headlines screamed that "Squeaky" Fromme, the woman who had tried to kill President Ford, had been arrested in Sacramento Friday; the same day busing of over 22,000 students had begun in Louisville; Chris Evert had beaten Evonne Goolagong in the U.S. Women's Open the day before; and an earthquake in Turkey had killed a thousand villagers.

Below the fold it was business as usual, with articles about a teachers' strike in Boonton and a threatened one in New York City, another case of child molestation, and a local pediatrician being honored next weekend. Wendy recognized a couple of the bylines as people she'd worked with.

Sometimes she missed all the bustle of the paper; other times, she was glad to be rid of it. Especially with all the depressing news—

[ 31 ]

and frankly, lately that's all there was, what with the protests about busings, the fall of Saigon, the highest U.S. unemployment rate since 1941, the disappearance of union leader Jimmy Hoffa, the acquittal of the governor of Ohio and members of the National Guard for the 1970 Kent State University campus killings, a world population now of four billion people, New York City just barely saved from bankruptcy, hijackings left and right, one natural disaster after another around the world—

Some good things must have happened? Yeah, name any five. She tried to think of something good that had happened during the year. There'd been the linkup of the Apollo and Soyuz spacecrafts in July; in essence the space race was over.

And? she prompted herself. And?

For the life of her, she couldn't think of anything else positive. That was pretty depressing in itself. Maybe she had gotten out of the newspaper business just in time.

She stuck the paper in her grocery sack and marched off to her car. She sighed when she once more looked at the grille.

# SIX

Once home, she made a note on the small chalkboard by the phone to call her insurance company in the morning to let them know what happened.

There goes my premium, she thought. She looked outside. The girl from next door was out playing again. Obviously she was an only child. Wendy sympathized immediately; she had just had the one brother, but she had always felt alone too.

The difference, though, was that she'd grown up in Hunters Heights and had never had to make new friends. This girl would need to find a whole new group.

There weren't as many neighborhood kids as there had been ten years ago or even when Wendy had been growing up in the neighborhood, but there were the Crawford kids up the block, and the Pascals three houses down, and none of them were too bad, although Sal Pascal tended to put cherry bombs in neighbors' curbside mailboxes around the Fourth of July, and she suspected that next year, what with the bicentennial celebration in full swing, he would really go to town with illegal fireworks. So far no one had been hurt, but there'd been a run on mailboxes at the local hardware store, and Mr. Ferguson was doing a booming business—as it were.

Right now the new girl was heading toward Wendy's gazebo. Usually she didn't like to encourage the neighborhood kids to play there—it was an old structure, and she wanted to make sure that it would last a good many more years—but she didn't see any harm this time. In fact, the girl was sitting down on the flagstone floor and reading a book she had brought with her.

Wendy checked her watch. 4:16. Too late to go upstairs and start work, then stop for dinner. It was so easy finding excuses, she thought with a grin.

Dudley, the black cocker, came padding down the stairs. She opened the back screen door and let him out. Of course, he made a beeline for the girl. As soon as he reached his prey Dudley started licking her face and hands, and Wendy could hear giggles.

She took out a bottle of Coke and went to the door.

"Hi there, new neighbor," she called. "Want to come in for a soda?"

The girl glanced at her house, then seemed to make up her mind. She jumped to her feet, the book still in her hand, and raced toward Wendy's door. Dudley followed, his long ears flapping.

"Hi. I'm Wendy Wallace," she said, extending her hand formally.

The child shook it solemnly as she came into the kitchen. "I'm Jessica Morrison. Everyone calls me Jessie. Except my mother, who calls me Jessica Mae." She wrinkled her nose to show what she thought about that.

Wendy smiled briefly. She remembered all too well how stuffy adults could be. "A Southerner, huh?"

The girl blushed. "Yeah, you must have heard my accent. I know it's real different."

"But nice."

"Yeah?" She almost smiled.

"Yeah. Sit down, Jessie. Do you like Coke or Seven-Up?"

"Coke would be nice, thank you." She sat at the kitchen table, setting her book down. Wendy saw that it was one of the Nancy Drew series. She had read them all, too, when she was that age. Jessie petted Dudley, who had taken an instant liking to his new friend. Of course, thought Wendy, Dudley liked everyone who looked in his direction. He even liked the mailman, which had to be a first for the dog world.

"Here you go." Wendy set two tumblers filled with cola down. "What about cookies?"

"My mom doesn't like me to have them very often. She wants me to snack on celery and things."

"Ugh," they both said at once, then laughed.

"I'll get the cookies." She brought out an unopened pack of chocolate chips and placed it on the table.

Finally, Wendy had a chance to study her visitor a bit as the girl sipped her soda and nibbled at a cookie. Jessie was blond, with her long hair trailing almost to her waist. She was slender, and a trifle awkward. Coltish, as if she was still growing into her body—which of course she was. The child's eyes were gray and large and rimmed with long dark lashes. Her nose was delicate, her skin tanned. She wore a red short-sleeved blouse and matching shorts. The chain she wore around her neck had slipped outside her blouse, and Wendy saw a bulky silver ring inset with a simple blue stone.

"That's a nice necklace."

Jessie touched it, as if realizing for the first time the chain and ring were showing. "The ring was my dad's." She fingered the stone, then thrust the necklace inside her shirt.

Was, Wendy noted. "I've been watching you move in. Is it just you and your mom and dad?"

"Me and my mother and my *stepfather*," Jessie corrected quietly.

"Ah yes. Just the three, huh?"

"Yeah." Her expression unreadable, Jessie looked down. "What's your dog's name?"

"Dudley Do Right, or Dudley for short. You know, after the Canadian Mountie in the cartoon."

"Oh yeah. I don't see much TV. My mom," she said simply, slightly raising one shoulder.

"He likes you." Wendy nodded to the dog, who kept giving Jessie his paw so that she could shake it. The girl giggled. Dudley cocked his head, and barked once.

"I like him. I'd like to have a cat or dog or hamster, even, but—"

Her mom, Wendy finished mentally. A firm mother, strict—perhaps too much so?

And here she was breeding dissension by giving the girl sodas and cookies and having her be with the dog. Oh well, some rules were meant to be broken. God knows, she thought with a rueful shake of her head, next she'd be teaching the girl to be a gunrunner. She almost laughed aloud.

Which reminded her for some reason of the scream she had thought she'd heard last night. Worried, she had called the police and they had sent a squad car by, but they hadn't found anything amiss up or down the block. Had the scream come from next door? Wendy wondered. It wasn't something she could ask Jessie at their first meeting.

Jessie shook Dudley's paw again. "Do you like squirrels?"

"Sure do. I have a feeder out back for them, and several for birds—you probably saw those out by the birdbath and the bushes—and during the summer I get some raccoon visitors as well."

[ 35 ]

"And you don't chase them away?" Jessie looked amazed.

"Nope. I like animals. I'm hoping to encourage a bunny I've seen the past month to come up to me, but I don't think he'll do it. I bet he's searching for a place to hang out for the winter."

"Wow." Jessie took a drink of her Coke and looked around at the kitchen.

The room was old-fashioned, never having been modernized. Wendy couldn't remember her parents ever making improvements to the house; her dad would fix what was broken, but that was it. After they had died and she had moved back to the house after her divorce, she had meant to update the room, but had never had the energy—or the money—to do so. The linoleum floor was old but still serviceable, if more than a little ugly. The stove was white and large and just this side of primitive, but it worked well enough for her meager needs. The refrigerator hummed more than it should, and she suspected it was on the verge of an imminent breakdown. However, the cabinets were oak and had glass insets in front, on which had been etched various flowers. A row of potted herbs lined the windowsill above the sink.

"This is nice," Jessie said, starting on another cookie. "Our kitchen is bigger, but it's not as . . . warm, I guess. It's got all this modern stuff in it. My mom likes to cook; she's always in the kitchen. We've got an ice maker, and all these electric gadgets. My dad used to tease her about her buying all these kitchen things."

Her father used to? Wendy said nothing.

"I like your colors better—blue and white. Ours are yellow and green. Yucky. I don't like to sit in it. We have a dining room anyway where we eat most times. Except breakfasts. We have to eat in the kitchen then, because Mom doesn't like a mess right off in the morning. She likes to keep the house pretty tidy. She doesn't touch my room, though she tries sometimes."

Strict, and fussy, too. Not sure I'm going to like this woman, Wendy thought. Of course, I shouldn't really prejudge her. Right? Uh-huh.

"How do you like the rest of your new house?" Wendy said, reaching for a cookie. She broke it in half and fed part to Dudley.

Jessie smiled down at Dudley, who sat gazing up at her, his tongue lolling. It was obvious he was hoping she'd drop part of a cookie so he could gobble it up. She shrugged offhandedly. "It's okay, I guess. It's bigger than where we used to live."

"Where was that?"

"Lexington." She paused. "That's in Kentucky."

"I was there once."

Jessie brightened. "Really? When?"

"About five years ago. I had a book that took place there, and I had to do some research."

"Really?" Jessie looked thoughtful for a moment. "You write books?" Wendy nodded. "Wow!"

Wendy waited for the inevitable and altogether silly questions: Are you famous? Have I read anything of yours? Are you published yet? Where do you get your ideas?

Jessie did better.

"Do you write books like this?" she said, pointing to her Nancy Drew.

"Well, I write mysteries for adults, actually, but I have done one young adult book. It's at my publisher's," she said.

"Could I see your office?" Jessie asked shyly. "I've never met a real writer before."

"Sure. Come on." Wendy snagged a cookie and led the way up the stairway and into the back room. "This is it," she said.

Jessie stared around. "It's really big."

Wendy had chosen the largest room, what had once been her parents' room, for the office; the next biggest bedroom had become hers. The other two, originally hers and her brother's, she used as spare rooms when company came. Hank wouldn't need his room again; he had died just months before the end of the war.

Jessie went up to the IBM Selectric sitting on the old pine desk and stared at it, then turned to the bookcases lining one wall.

"Those are yours, right?" She pointed to a line of books atop the closest bookcase.

"Right. Those are the covers of my novels on this wall." She had had each book cover matted and framed. So far, there were nine. The tenth—the young adult book—was at her publisher's right now and she was working on number eleven.

"How come you have nuns on your covers?"

"Because my books have continuing characters in them—two nuns named Sister Rosalie and Sister Mary Michael."

"Oh. I don't know any nuns. Do you?"

"I did when I was a child. My teachers were all nuns."

"Like the nuns in your books?"

"Well, the real nuns weren't quite as agreeable as mine, unfortunately."

"Probably made you eat celery, huh?"

"You got it."

They both chuckled.

Now Jessie was studying the titles in the occult section of Wendy's research library on the other side of the room. She touched the spine of a book entitled *Magic: Practikal Uses and Applications*.

"Do you know anything about spells?" she asked.

"What kind of spells?"

"Um, I'm not sure. Just, uh, spells."

"A little. Do you want to borrow the book and look something up?"

Jessie smiled eagerly, then her expression became bland as she glanced out the window toward her house. "Well, maybe later."

The mother again, Wendy thought, who knew she would absolutely not get along with this woman at all. Probably censored everything her child read, and Wendy wondered how it was that Jessie was reading Nancy Drew mysteries. She was surprised the mother hadn't discovered something objectionable in them. Maybe Nancy uttered a "darn" or "drat" once or twice.

Give her time, she thought.

"Sure. Any time."

Jessie wandered from room to room, just looking into each briefly. Wendy didn't mind. Obviously the kid needed to get away from her mother for a while, and curiosity was healthy, right? Right.

Jessie paused at the door of the bathroom. It was cozy, with a big tub taking up one end of the room.

"Um, would you mind, Miss Wallace, if I came over some night and took a bath?"

Wendy was startled; she'd never had anyone request a bath in her house before. "Well, sure. Don't you have a bath at home, though?"

"No. Just a shower, and . . . well . . . I don't like it much."

"Any time you want to come over, go ahead. The back door is always unlocked."

Jessie's head jerked up at the sound of a door slamming next door.

"Jessica Mae! Jessica Mae!"

"I gotta go. Thanks for the stuff." She ran down the stairs, Wendy following, and instead of going out the back door where her mother would see her coming out of a neighbor's house, Jessie slipped quickly out the front.

Wendy paused in the dining room and watched as the girl went around her house to the back.

"Hi, Mom." Jessie sounded fairly casual.

Would her mother fall for it? Wendy wondered.

Jessie's mother whirled around, and Wendy could see the woman was frowning. She couldn't see a great deal more because of the rose of Sharon blooming on that side of the house. It was nice for privacy—but not when you wanted to spy on the neighbors.

"Haven't you heard me just callin' and callin' you, Jessica Mae? I've been out here for*ever*. Wherever were you?"

The mother's accent was far stronger than her daughter's, and it was obvious where Jessie got her hair and eyes.

"Well?" The word was drawn out, almost two or three syllables.

Jessie nodded vaguely toward the front of the house with her head.

Not quite a lie, Wendy thought ironically.

"Well, come on inside now, Jessica Mae. It's almost time for dinner, and you have to get washed up and set the table, and I nearly burned the roast while I was out lookin' for you. Now, don't you go and be givin' me a headache today, all right? I am feelin' mighty achy anyway with this awful heat." Without looking back, the mother pivoted around and went inside.

Jessie started to follow, then turned to look up into the dining-room windows, as if she knew Wendy would be standing there. She put a finger to her lips.

A sad little gesture, Wendy thought, and waved. Then the girl went inside, and Wendy was wondering what kind of neighbors she had now, although surely anything would be better than those dreadful people who had lived there before and who had fought constantly and loudly and who had the motorcycles and worked on them at all hours of the night.

Once again she wondered if the screaming came from that house. Was the mother a child beater? Was the husband the culprit?

Strange.

Almost as strange as her run-in that afternoon. She'd met two new people today, and she much preferred the child over the rude adult.

Break's over. Back to work again. As she passed the bathroom, she remembered again Jessie's request about using the bathtub.

Curiouser and curiouser, she thought, then turned to her typewriter and thought no more of her neighbors.

# SEVEN

During dinner Jessie didn't mention meeting their neighbor. She knew that her mother wouldn't approve of Wendy.

Miss Wallace, that is. Or maybe it was Mrs. Wallace, although come to think of it, the woman hadn't mentioned a husband. Maybe she was divorced. Or widowed.

Jessie swallowed quickly.

"What's wrong?" her mother asked anxiously.

"Nothing."

"For God's sake, Astrid, leave the kid alone." Patrick was shoveling food into his mouth as if this was his only concern in the world, and this was the first time since sitting down at the dining-room table ten minutes ago that he had spoken. He hadn't met Jessie's eye earlier in the day, either. Things had been fairly quiet today with her mother and stepfather putting more things in order around the house, which was why she had decided to go outside. It was better to be outside, away from them, away from the strange silence.

The three of them hadn't spoken much to each other since she'd started screaming yesterday. Patrick had quickly stepped out of the shower, slapped her once on the face, and Jessie had stopped screaming.

Then she had gone into the shower and stood, silent, while the hurtful water pounded down on her, and the pain welled up inside. She had bit her lip, not screaming, not whimpering, not making a single sound. Just enduring.

Afterward as she had dried herself off with her pink towel, she had seen Patrick watching her.

"See now, that wasn't so bad, was it?" He had tried to smile, but his expression was sickly. His face looked ashen, like he had lost his tan all at once. His glance slid away from hers.

Jessie had said nothing. She had simply left the bathroom, gone into her bedroom, put on the T-shirt her father had won for her at a county fair a couple of years ago, which she used as a nightgown, and crawled into bed.

Her mother had not come in to kiss her good night.

She knew her mother went to bed with a headache, brought on by "that ungrateful child."

That was her: Jessie, the ungrateful child. She had heard her mother call her that more than once, even when her father was alive. Her father had been able to divert her mother's attention from her, though; Patrick couldn't. Jessie sighed. She knew her mother loved her—well, she *supposed* she did—but she had a mighty peculiar way of showing it.

Now Jessie looked up from her plate and saw that Patrick had been staring at her again. He glanced down immediately at his dinner. Her mother ignored them both and continued to pick at her food.

They ate their slices of slightly underdone—a far cry from nearly burned—roast in silence. Jessie wished they could have something like a salad or sliced fruit when it got this hot, but her mother insisted on making a proper Southern Sunday dinner, because that was what her mother had done, and her mother's mother before her. So they had a big meal every Sunday night in the winter, autumn, spring, and summer. And that was just the way it was. Jessie bet that Miss Wallace had salads or cold cuts, something good.

Jessie pushed a piece of carrot around with her fork, caught Patrick's eye on her again, speared the vegetable, and popped it in her mouth. She concentrated on chewing.

"You got everything ready for the big day tomorrow?" he asked.

The Big Day. Her stomach tightened. Her first day at the Hunters Heights Junior High School. She could just hear the comments. "Lookit the cracker." Except that she supposed these kids wouldn't know what a "cracker" was, and technically, of course, she wasn't one.

She pointed to her mouth to indicate it was full, and there was just one more thing that her mother absolutely would not tolerate and that was speaking with your mouth full of food. Patrick had already found that out when he was first dating her mom.

Patrick nodded.

[ 41 ]

When she could speak, Jessie said, slicing a chunk of potato in half, "I got my clothes all ready."

"What're you wearing?" he asked.

"Why, Patrick, she is wearin' what every child will be wearin'— her best clothes."

"I don't think they do that anymore, Astrid," he said, with a wink to Jessie.

For a moment she almost liked him again. Then it was gone.

"Yeah," Patrick said, "things have really changed. I've seen them in shorts and jeans and T-shirts and all sorts of weird stuff."

"My daughter," she said stiffly, "is not goin' to school in cutoffs like some sharecropper's daughter. Or worse, some *Negro*."

Patrick said nothing.

Jessie had had this fight with her mother before. "Mom, I told you. They're called blacks or Afro-Americans now. Not that word."

"I know perfectly well what *they* are called, Jessica Mae, and where I come from—and where you do too, missy—they are Negroes. Or the colored. Or worse. Take your pick." She scowled at her daughter, her lips pressed together. "I will not stand for you correctin' me. It's not proper."

Jessie said nothing.

"Now, what about your clothin'?"

"I have my new shoes, a good pair of pants, and that new blouse you bought me, Mom."

"I do wish you would wear a dress. It is ever so much more ladylike."

Jessie said nothing; her mother knew it was useless to argue about that. She wouldn't wear a dress. Period.

Her mother was frowning. "Which blouse is that?"

"The pink one."

The crease between her mother's eyes disappeared. "That's good."

Of course, everything that her mother bought her was pink or lavender or yellow. She would have liked to get something else. Something blue, maybe, or green. Or even black. White, too, that would be nice. Although her mother thought she should only wear white when they went to church—which was rarely now that her father had died—and wouldn't allow her to wear it otherwise because she insisted that Jessie would just get stains all over it anyway.

"Do you know what classes you'll have?" Patrick asked. He had finished his roast and potatoes and was having seconds. He hadn't had any carrots, and Jessie just knew her mother would point that out in a minute or so. She wondered what difference it made if he didn't eat the carrots.

"No. I'll find out tomorrow. I'm supposed to be in that advanced art class." She glanced sideways at her mother. Silence. That was good. Her mom had opposed her taking the art course, and she didn't really know why. Who knew why her mother objected to things? She just did.

"Well, that's good. I won't have a long day tomorrow, it being my first day back. Want me to pick you up at school?"

"Thanks, but I'll just walk. It's not that far."

"Okay." He looked down at his plate.

She sighed to herself. She should have let him pick her up. It was too late to change things now.

Her mother shoved her plate away, then stood, the legs of the chair scraping on the bare floor.

"I have a headache," she announced, and she left the dining room without a further word.

"We'll do the dishes, right, kiddo?" Patrick said with another wink, as if he were Jessie's best buddy.

"Right."

She wished he wouldn't try to be so cheerful. It made him sound worse. It almost made him likable.

They finished their meal without speaking, and then Jessie went out into the kitchen and brought out the bowls of tapioca her mother had made earlier. Patrick had two, and so did she.

Then, still without speaking, they washed the dishes in the stainless-steel sink and cleaned the dining room table, and politely she said good night to him and went upstairs.

Tonight, Jessie noticed, he had not insisted that she take a shower. Good. She couldn't have taken that again. Not so soon.

She tiptoed past her mother's room, the one that she shared with Patrick—she didn't have to worry about making noise, though, because the door was shut—and went into hers, down the hall, far away from them.

She closed the door and crossed to the windowseat in the dark, playing with the ring on the chain as she did so, sliding it back and forth. She could see Miss—Mrs?—Wallace's office from here. Jessie checked the clock. It was almost eight, and her friend was still at work. Jessie guessed that writers must work awfully late.

She yawned.

[ 43 ]

Time to go to bed. She set her alarm. She had to get up early for school. Her stomach knotted again. Her mother had already offered to take her to school, but Jessie didn't want her to.

It was bad enough to go to a new school, worse to have your mom take you, like you were some kindergarten baby or something.

She touched the stuffed animals—a polar bear and a brown cat—on her dresser, felt the leather top of her small jewelry case. Sometimes she liked to move around the room and just touch things; she liked the textures—the fuzziness of the cat, the softness of the jewel box her dad had brought to her from one of his trips, the cold hardness of her grandmother's silver comb and hairbrush—

She undressed quickly, put on her T-shirt, then turned on the overhead light and inspected the clothes that she had laid out across the back of the ladder-backed wooden chair she and her dad had painted bright red, which her mother insisted was simply vulgar. Her mother had set it out on the curb for the trashmen when they were moving, but Jessie had rescued it, and nothing had been said about it since. She checked to make sure she had spiral notebooks and pencils and pens in various colors, and that the pink—of course—three-ring notebook filled with paper that her mother had bought for her was in the canvas school bag.

She had already checked these items earlier today and yesterday as well, but she just wanted to make sure everything was really there. Can't leave any loose ends flapping in the breeze, as her father used to say.

Used to say.

Her face started to crinkle up. No, she told herself. No. Not tonight. No, no, no. . .

She wiped a hand across her eyes and crawled into bed, remembered the light, and got out to turn it off. Once again in bed, she lay down, her fingers laced behind her head, and realized she could see the writer's window from here. The light was reassuring.

She wished she could feel excited about going to school. She used to. Long before her dad died and Patrick came and they moved here.

Now, all she had inside was what felt like a hard knot in her stomach.

The shadows of a tree's interwoven leaves fell across one of her still-bare walls, and she watched them flicker. The wind must be coming up. Today while she was out she had noticed some of the leaves turning color. Most were still green, but some were yellow now, some red. Maybe she could find a handful of the better ones and make a collection of them. She could identify each leaf on a piece of notebook paper, and write about the trees—which ones acorns came from and which had those funny whirligig seeds. That would be neat. Maybe that could be a science project. She could draw them too, and what the trees looked like. There wasn't anything she couldn't draw, she decided.

She yawned again.

The wall, she promised herself, wouldn't be bare for long. She'd make a picture in art class and hang it up there. Maybe Wendy would like one of her drawings for one of her walls.

Jessie thought she heard the momentary rise of voices down the hall, and stiffened. Probably not. She hadn't been able to hear them talking or anything else in this house, which was good, because in the apartment she had and it was sickening. She had slammed the pillow over her ears, but she still could hear things. And she didn't like it. Her dad wouldn't have liked it.

A toilet flushed, and she knew Patrick would be going to bed soon. He didn't usually go to bed so early, but she knew he must be nervous about his first day; he had to leave real early to get to nearby New York City on time. He had worked in this office before being transferred down South, but he said things had changed since he'd left.

Something flicked against the screen.

Just a moth probably. They had big ones down in Lexington. Scorpions, too. Her mother had like to fainted the time she'd found a scorpion and the husks of two spiders in a corner of Jessie's bedroom.

Jessie grinned. She had thought the bugs were neat. Really neat.

The light in Wendy's office winked out.

Jessie raised herself up on her elbows, and saw a light go on downstairs in the back of the house. The kitchen. Maybe Wendy was going to have her dinner now. Or a snack. Jessie checked the luminous dial of her round clock. It was nearly nine. An odd hour for dinner, but she guessed that writers did strange things at odd times. Artists did, too.

Which was why she was going to be an artist when she grew up, just like her dad was until her mom forced him to give up his art and get what she called a "real job." Jessie was going to be an artist, and live the bohemian life—she'd read that phrase somewhere—and she was going to do really different things which would just drive her mother crazy. She'd really wring her hands then. No one would be able to stop her because she would be an artist and she'd get lots of money for her paintings.

She lay back down and drew the sheet up to her chin. It was cool tonight, far cooler than it had been the past few nights, which was good. She didn't like it when it was so hot; she didn't sleep well then. Her quilt with its bright reds and blues, which Grandmother Morrison had made by hand, was folded neatly across the foot of her bed. Ready to use when it got cold. She was looking forward to all the snow she had read about.

It would be nice to have a pet curling up on her bed now. She wished she could borrow Dudley. That would be pleasant to have a little warm thing snuggled up against her, something she could reach out to and touch for reassurance when she woke up in the dark.

Maybe someday.

Maybe when she was an artist. Then she'd have dozens of cats and dogs, and probably her mother would never come to visit her.

She closed her eyes and listened to the night sounds of the tree frogs peeping; from the yard came the hooting of an owl, and high up the eerie honking of Canada geese. A dog bayed somewhere. Another, much farther away, echoed the barks, but in a deeper voice.

Soon she was asleep, and the night sounds went on around her.

# EIGHT

"Another cup of coffee, Herr Marek?" the woman in the frilly purple dress simpered. Her round face was coarsely powdered, and she had a heavy hand with eye makeup. However, she did make a delicious dinner of roast chicken with tarragon, and new potatoes with dill. He couldn't fault her on that. On the other hand—

Stefan Marek's lips pressed together. Several times he had told the woman he wasn't German, that he was Czech, but she insisted on addressing him as "Herr." It was probably, he thought, the only thing she understood.

"No, thank you, Mrs. Addison. I've had quite enough, and believe me, I would like to sleep tonight."

The simper deepened.

"And the peach cobbler was delicious."

"Thank you," she cooed. "I only pick the ripest ones, you know."

"I have no doubt."

The couple across from him rolled their eyes in sympathy. He hid a smile. The man to his right stiffened and gave him a sidelong glance. Probably thought he was making a pass at the old woman.

When Marek had phoned his Uncle Karel to say he would be arriving in the States, he'd told his relative that he needed some place where he could come and go in Hunters Heights easily. Karel, who had a wife and five children and not enough space in his two-story house, out in the development adjacent to the glassworks, had suggested the newly refurbished Addison Bed-and-Breakfast, and Marek had made his reservations.

What Karel had neglected—either deliberately or through actual ignorance—to tell him was that the proprietor, who had to be eighty-seven if she were a day, was a gossipy old bag.

Well, perhaps that wasn't so bad, after all. He was there, in a way, to listen to gossip, and who should know more about the goings-on in this town than this old lady, who had lived here all her life?

Several times since his arrival Marek had tried to draw her out about the town. It had proved successful beyond his wildest expectations. She had talked all day, off and on, about Hunters Heights— who had settled when, who had married whom, who'd had an unexpected child late in life.

"Just what is it you do for a living, Herr Marek?" Mrs. Addison asked.

"I'm a journalist," he replied, "for *Praha Zprávy*. The *Prague Bulletin*," he translated.

"Prague? That in Poland?" a businessman type in a lime green leisure suit and unshaved jowls asked.

"Czechoslovakia."

He had seen the blank looks; less was known about his country than either of its larger neighbors, Poland or the Soviet Union. Either someone called him a Pole or a Russkie, and then promptly told him a Polish joke in incredibly poor taste. He was used to it. That didn't mean he liked it, though.

Someone now was tapping the front section of the Sunday *Herald-Journal*.

". . . isn't it?" Mrs. Addison was saying, her eyelashes fluttering. "We're *so* very proud of him. He's *absolutely* wonderful, you know. I wish I were under thirteen, then he could be my doctor."

The guests gathered around the dining room table politely chuckled.

"He's very handsome," she said, commenting on the picture in the newspaper. She brushed at a ruffle on her dress. "So much better looking than Mr. Addison, who while he was a good soul, you know, really wasn't much in the looks department."

"Indeed, he is quite distinguished," Marek said, glancing at the grainy newspaper picture of the physician who was to be honored. The man, while obviously in his late sixties, could well have passed for a man ten years younger.

Mrs. Addison glanced at him, her lips pursed. "You find him attractive, Herr Marek?"

He knew what she was hinting at. Apparently Mrs. Addison didn't settle for knowing less than a full history of her guests' sexual and financial history. Nosy was too mild a word for her.

[ 48 ]

"What I mean to say is that I only hope I look half as good when I am his age."

Her obviously fake eyelashes—one of them was coming unglued, but so far she hadn't noticed—rippled in what he guessed she thought was a highly seductive display. "Oh, I'm sure you will."

He decided to keep quiet.

Conversation turned to the bicentennial celebration, which had officially begun in March and would last for twenty-two long months through 1975 *and* '76—of course, Marek thought, what else do Americans talk of these days? He and the others talked about the assassination attempt on the president's life by one of Charles Manson's so-called Family, and Mrs. Addison said tearfully it reminded her of those awful days after JFK had been shot. Marek observed to himself that President Ford could hardly be compared to President Kennedy.

The couple across from him and the man in the green leisure suit talked of the weather in the state—the dry summer, then the series of downbursts which had destroyed so many crops. Someone asked him how he felt about that Czech woman defecting—was he planning on doing that? Was that why he was here?

Somehow, through all the topics of weather and sports and politics, the conversation worked its way around to Israel. Israel, it seemed, was always in the news, and never far from the minds of Americans. Mrs. Addison and several of the men were adamantly opposed to additional U.S. aid to the Middle Eastern country. The young couple maintained Israel had every right to it, after what the people there had gone through. Marek wisely maintained his silence.

"Those damned Jews," said a man at one end of the table, who was not much older than Marek and who should have known better. "They always want money and more money."

Marek set his nearly empty coffee cup down carefully on its hand-painted china saucer.

"Yeah, we just pour millions and millions into that desert, and what do we get? Nothing," said the man in the leisure suit.

"The Jews own the banks, you know, Mr. Galton," Mrs. Addison said in a confiding tone. "I've read that there's this international conspiracy of Jews attempting to take over the financial industry— and well, you know, they're in the publishing and movie industry as well—and put all the Christians out of business. And you know the man who foreclosed on the Catholic school over in Mapleton

[ 49 ]

last month, well, he was a Jew. You know how much they hate the Catholics."

Marek couldn't take it any more. "Mrs. Addison," he said, rising to his feet and looking down at her, "I am a Jew."

The gasp she gave as he went through the doorway almost made him smile.

He knew what she and the others at the table would be saying now that he was gone. He doesn't look . . . you couldn't tell . . . but his nose is so small. . . . He looks more like a Gypsy, don't you think . . . ?

All the thoughtless stupid things that people had said over and over, all through the years. What a surprise when they found he was a Jew; why, he didn't look like the stereotype at all. Where were those long locks, Herr Marek? Aren't you a banker? Aren't all Jews rich? Most of the time these things weren't said maliciously; they were uttered in profound ignorance. Sometimes he wondered if that wasn't worse.

His lip curled as he stepped out onto the front porch for some fresh air.

From here he had a good view of downtown, such as it was. He could see the bank, the post office, a department store, Ferguson's Hardware, two restaurants, and beyond that the road that led to the clinic where five doctors, including the one who was to be honored next Saturday, had offices.

Marek sat on the railing and smoked a cigarette.

It was almost dark, and he could see the lights coming on in the town. Next door, lights flicked on, and he looked that way; as he did, his gaze fell on the rented Buick and he sighed, remembering the accident yesterday afternoon.

He'd been pretty hard on her, particularly since the accident had messed up his immediate plans. The misadventure was as much his fault as hers, to be honest. He had just been lucky the police officer hadn't ticketed him as well. He didn't need that kind of attention.

When he finished the cigarette he went back inside the bed-and-breakfast, but found the dining room empty. He went up the stairway to his bedroom, listened for a moment, and, when he heard nothing, went in and locked the door.

Jessie's eyes fluttered open.

Something was rustling beneath her windows.

What was that? She listened. The rustling grew louder.

She couldn't just lie in bed, not knowing what was making the noise. She wasn't a sissy. Probably her mom would be fainting by now, sure that it was someone come to break in and steal everything and beat them up, or even worse, kill them.

Jessie knew better.

She pushed the sheet back and crept over to the window seat. She stared down, not sure what to expect.

Light in Wendy's kitchen spilled out onto the small patio in back and onto her drive, which ran between the two houses. A moment later Jessie saw a fat raccoon waddling toward a pan set a few feet away from the door. Wendy had put out the raccoon's food.

Grinning, Jessie watched the animal gobble his tidbits. He kept looking around, as if he almost expected someone—or something—to rush out of the darkness and grab his meal. When nothing more was forthcoming, the raccoon ambled off to the opposite side of the house, the bushes crackling as he pushed through them.

She returned to bed. Silly her. All that noise . . . and here it was nothing more than a half-tame animal. She guessed she was going to have to get used to that sound.

The owl hooted again.

The tree frogs stopped peeping.

She closed her eyes, and her breathing evened out, and she fell into the grayness. She clawed at its alienness, but her fingers just went through it without stopping her at all, and she slid down and down and down, whirling through the grayness. She screamed, but no one could hear her because everyone around her was screaming as well, and she could smell urine and sweat and worse things, and felt the thrashing arms and legs against her, and tasted the vomit rising in her throat, and she knew if she threw up she would get beaten, and she couldn't couldn't *couldn't* take the pain much longer, and they were moving, shuffling naked through the suffocating grayness, the hissing of the shower growing louder—

Jessie woke, sitting bolt upright in bed and screaming, though she made no sound. She shuddered so hard the bed rocked, feeling nauseated, afraid to move, to call out for her mother. Sweat trickled down her face, plastering a strand of limp hair to her cheek. She could feel the dampness along her back, down into her panties, and knew she must stink from it.

But she couldn't do anything.

Slowly, agonizingly, the minutes ticked away, and she didn't move; she was too fearful.

The light in Wendy's kitchen went out sometime after two in the morning, as did all the ones downstairs and upstairs, and still Jessie sat up in bed, not moving.

She wanted her mother, her father; she wanted someone's arms around her, wanted a reassuring hug.

No one came.

She was alone. All alone.

Finally, when the nausea went away, when she could no longer smell the awful things, could no longer hear the screams and cries and whimpering, when she didn't think the grayness would come back to enfold her in its suffocating grasp, she eased herself down onto the damp mattress and pulled the sheet over her trembling body.

But she did not close her eyes, and she did not sleep for the rest of the night.

# MONDAY

# NINE

In the morning Jessie woke up with a sore throat. At least she thought it was a sore throat. It *might* be one by midday; you could never tell.

Patrick had already left for work—he said the commute into New York City was long—and so there was just her and her mom. Still in her T-shirt, she headed downstairs.

"Mom?"

She trailed through the rooms, thinking how empty they were compared to the house next door. The furniture was all here, but it wasn't a home. Not really.

"Mom?"

No answer.

She peered into her mother's room—she couldn't think of it as her mom's and Patrick's room—and saw her, still in bed, with a sheet pulled over her.

"Mom?"

Astrid Fields moaned in answer.

Jessie went in and stood by the bed and gazed down at her. Her mom never looked that good in morning light; you could see the fine wrinkles around her eyes and the lines around her lips that would make them pucker in years to come. In the morning, before her mother got dressed and put her makeup on, she always appeared ten years older. For some reason she didn't understand, that made Jessie sad.

As if sensing someone was there, Astrid opened one eye. It was bloodshot.

"Oh, Jessie," she said and waved a vague hand. "I just can't get up today, honey. It's my head; it feels like someone's hammerin' away in it. I was just so sick durin' the night. I'm sorry, but you'll have to get ready on your own."

"Okay, Mom. I hope you feel better." Jessie decided not to say anything about her own illness.

Astrid had already rolled over, though, and seemed to have forgotten about her daughter.

For a moment longer Jessie stood there and then went into her room. She stood at the window and watched as two squirrels chased each other through her yard and then into Wendy's; Dudley stood at the back door and barked at them.

She didn't know what to do. Her throat hurt even more than it had a few minutes ago, and now she had a bit of a stomachache too. Maybe she was getting some kind of flu or something.

She stood for a few minutes more, then decided she would get dressed. She put on jeans and a casual shirt and her good tennis shoes and then went downstairs to have breakfast. She poked at her cereal, but she didn't feel much like eating. The milk didn't taste right, either, and normally she loved milk.

Finally, she got up and put her house key in her jeans pocket, locked the door, and went outside. Her mother wouldn't miss her, she knew.

She knocked at Wendy's back door. The interior door was open, with just the screen closed. The dog barked when he saw her.

Wendy came in from another room. "Hi, there, Jessie, how are you?" She was already opening the door to let Jessie in.

"Hi, Miss Wallace."

"I thought you'd be on your way to school by now."

Jessie shifted from one foot to another.

Wendy peered at her. "Is something wrong?"

Jessie's words ran together. "I woke up with a sore throat, and now my tummy hurts, and my stepfather left early, and my mom is sick in bed with a headache." Patrick would have called her a baby, if he were home, and told her the sore throat and tummyache was all in her head. Didn't he understand? It wasn't!

Wendy looked serious. "I see. You know, you might have that bug that's going around."

Jessie just nodded.

"Would you like me to take you to your doctor?"

"I don't want to be a bother, Miss Wallace."

"You certainly aren't that, Jessie. Let me just run a comb

through my hair and we'll be on our way. What's your doctor's name?"

"We don't have a doctor here yet. That was somethin' my mom was going to do this week, only I don't think she's going to get around to it."

"Well, you know, my doctor doesn't take kid patients, but I know of a really good doctor in town. He's that guy who's getting the award this weekend. Maybe you saw him on the news?"

Jessie nodded, even though she didn't know what Wendy was talking about. She figured that Wendy knew that, but was just too polite to say anything. Unlike other adults Jessie had met, Wendy, she suspected, probably wouldn't criticize her or nag her. She wished she had Wendy as mother instead. Then she realized what she had thought and felt bad. Her mother couldn't help being the way she was.

Jessie patted Dudley while she waited for Wendy. A few minutes later the woman came back into the kitchen.

"I just called and explained the situation to his receptionist, and she says we can come in as soon as we get there."

Jessie nodded.

"I guess we ought to go now, although it's not that far away."

Jessie nodded again.

"Do you have to go and tell your mother?"

"No. She's asleep. She won't know."

*If I'm here or not . . .* they both could hear the unspoken words.

"Okay, so the animals are already fed, and we're on our way." Wendy grabbed her purse from a kitchen chair where it had been slung over the back, and retrieved her car keys.

She locked the door after they went out onto the porch and they walked over to the Rabbit.

Jessie didn't say anything on the way to the doctor's office; she just stared out the window, as the trees flashed by. Not for the first time she remembered that it was her first day of school. School. How excited she used to get about it . . . when her dad was still alive.

Just beyond the square, Wendy drove for a few minutes along the main road, then the car slowed and Wendy turned into a driveway of a sprawling one-story building. A number of cars were parked in the big lot already, and one was occupied.

Jessie glanced at the dark blue car, but the man inside had his head down, reading something on the seat beside him. Probably waiting for someone inside to finish their appointment. Sometimes her dad had sat outside and waited for her mom; that way, he said, he could listen to the radio. Her mother had thought it meant he hadn't cared. But he *had* cared about her; Jessie knew, even though her mother was always sick with a headache and something like that.

Inside the waiting room were a number of couches and chairs. Along one wall was a window with a sliding pane, and behind that sat several women. Jessie could see one typing. Nurses and stuff, she figured. A few patients sat around, leafing through magazines. After Wendy explained who they were, the receptionist handed her a small clipboard and a form to fill out, and they sat on the comfortable chairs.

Wendy asked Jessie some questions about illnesses she had had for the form, then handed it back to the receptionist. Then they sat again.

What Jessie really liked about Wendy was that the woman didn't seem compelled like so many adults to continually talk to her—as if there was a need to fill the silence with words. Sometimes, she knew, it was okay just to sit and not say a thing and it didn't mean you were mad or anything; her dad had taught her that.

Wendy picked up a copy of *Time* and began reading. She glanced up at Jessie and smiled reassuringly. Jessie smiled back. She found a copy of a children's magazine and flipped through it. She watched as an interior door, on the same wall as the sliding glass, opened, and a stout unsmiling woman in a white uniform called a name. A man with a limp and a little boy on the verge of tears headed toward her. The door closed behind them.

Jessie watched the remaining kids, two of them, somewhat younger than she. One of them didn't move, just sat there with his eyes closed. He must be really sick. The second kid, a girl, wiggled around and whined to her mother. Her mother was very patient with her daughter and read to her in a low voice. After a while the little girl turned around and hugged her mother and gave her a kiss. Jessie knew her mother would have just told her to stop squirming because it was giving her a headache. Her eyes bleared over suddenly and she glanced down at her magazine.

"Everything okay?" Wendy asked.

Jessie nodded, not trusting her voice.

Finally the boy went in, and then the other girl, and then it was her turn.

Wendy took her by the hand and led her into the doctor's office, which was through one door and down a short corridor to the right. Wendy sat in the doctor's office while Jessie stood and inspected all the framed certificates and awards; one wall had nothing but bookshelves and thick, important-looking books on it. There were lots of photos on the walls, too, of a tall man with various people, probably some of them mayors and governors and maybe even Presidents, she decided. In some of the photos he wasn't all that old, but she could see he got older through a number of them.

As Jessie stared at the photos, she felt something icy clutch like a hand at her stomach, and for the first time that day she really did have a bad stomachache. She could feel her legs trembling, and abruptly she plopped down in the chair next to Wendy.

"Okay?"

Jessie nodded. She felt as if something was pushing against her chest, as if she couldn't breathe, and she could feel the gray mist surrounding her—not here, not here, she cried silently, and in her head the clamor of the voices of old men and young women and children grew louder, and she was overwhelmed by the stench and stink of dirty, unwashed bodies, feeling the press of human flesh, the heat of the bodies suffocating her, and heard a door slamming and—

The doctor's office door slammed shut.

"I'm sorry to keep you ladies waiting," a man's voice said in an amiable tone, and Jessie's head snapped up.

"I'm Dr. Emerson Thorne." He extended his hand. "And you are?"

"Wendy Wallace. And this is my neighbor, Jessica Morrison, who's new in town. She doesn't feel too well today, and I thought I had better bring her in. I know there's a bug going around and I don't want her first week of school to get wrecked because of it."

"Excellent reasoning," the man said as he eased himself behind the huge oak desk and scanned the form Wendy had filled out with Jessie's help.

Wendy took the opportunity to study the pediatrician. He was slim and handsome with what could have been an actor's face, hair that had turned silver, not too short, and moderate sideburns. He was clean-shaven. His fingers were long, his hands well manicured—those of an artist, she thought. He had to be in his sixties, yet he was hardly a doddering old man. His manner could well have been that of a man twenty years younger. His voice was deep and well modulated, and there was just the faintest of accents, although she couldn't distinguish what kind. Very Continental, she told herself; very attractive.

"I see. It's always hard moving from one state to another; it's easy to get tired and then get some sort of virus." He smiled reassuringly. "And how are you feeling now, Miss Morrison?" He stared at her; not blinking, then finally glanced down at the folder on his desk.

Jessie said nothing, and Wendy glanced at her. She knew the girl was shy, and coming to a strange doctor was always a hard experience.

Jessie was staring at Dr. Thorne; Wendy realized the girl was trembling. Wendy touched Jessie's arm and she started, as if she had just remembered the woman was there.

"Jessie, are you all right?"

Slowly Jessie nodded. She was still looking at Dr. Thorne. Wendy saw how pale the girl was, and for a moment she thought Jessie was about to faint.

# TEN

"Perhaps it would be best if you waited outside, Miss Wallace," Dr. Thorne said.

Wendy frowned, a trifle reluctant. "I don't know. Jessie doesn't really know anyone, and I did bring her."

He smiled. "It will be quite all right, I assure you, Miss Wallace. After all, I am a children's doctor."

"Okay. I'll be out in the waiting room, if you need me, Jessie."

Jessie nodded again. Her hands were on either side of her legs, clenching the seat of the chair so hard her knuckles were white.

The door shut behind Wendy, and Jessie was alone with Dr. Thorne.

The smile on Thorne's face faded to an expression of concern.

"Is there something that you would like to talk to me about, Jessie? Something about your move from Kentucky, perhaps, or your first day of school?"

She shook her head.

"How is your stomach now?"

Nothing.

"Do you have a headache?"

Nothing.

He should take her into the examination room. Nothing would be accomplished here—he could ask her sixty, seventy questions, and he suspected he wouldn't get a response. He opened the door to another room and said, "Why don't you come in here, Jessie?"

She looked at him, then at the room beyond, and opened her mouth wide, though no sound came out, and he knew that she was screaming. She was pretty, he thought, quite pretty; it was a shame that you couldn't see it for the peculiar expression on her face now. Frowning, he buzzed the nurse.

"Mrs. Peterson, I'm having some trouble with this child. She won't talk to me. Perhaps you can do better."

"Of course, Doctor," came the tinny voice.

A moment later the stout woman dressed in white entered the doctor's office.

"I'll look at you, honey," she said in the cloying tones adults often use with children.

Jessie said nothing, but allowed herself to be led into the examining room. Mrs. Peterson examined her throat and ears, listened to her lungs with a stethoscope, and took her temperature and blood pressure. All the while Dr. Thorne stood in the doorway silently and watched the procedure; several times he made suggestions. Jessie never took her eyes off him.

Mrs. Peterson put away the stethoscope and frowned slightly. "Her lungs are clear; her temperature is normal, and so's her blood pressure. I can't find anything wrong, Doctor. She seems to be all right. She is kind of pale, though. I wonder if we should run some blood tests or something."

His eyes met those of Jessie's, and he felt something—something stir inside him, something he couldn't put a name to.

For a moment he said nothing. "No, I don't think so. All right, Mrs. Peterson, just tell the woman out there that I didn't find anything wrong with the child. It could just be nervous exhaustion from her move."

"Of course, Doctor."

The waiting room door slammed open and Jessie burst through it.

"What's wrong?" Wendy was on her feet.

Jessie flung her arms around her. Wendy stroked her hair and looked up at the nurse, who had followed Jessie at a slower pace.

"The doctor couldn't find anything wrong," she said gruffly. "Maybe she ought to stay home from school today, just in case."

"That's what I thought," Wendy said. Quickly she paid for the examination; she didn't want them to bill Jessie's mother. She had a feeling the woman would be upset that Wendy had brought her daughter to the doctor. Yet what was she supposed to do?

She saw the doctor down the hall and waved to him; he didn't wave back.

Odd, she thought, and then she stepped outside, Jessie following. As she crossed the parking lot and looked around, less intent than she had been when they'd gone in an hour ago, she caught sight of a familiar dark blue Buick. She stopped for a moment, then marched over to it.

"You," she said in an accusing tone.

Stefan Marek casually put down the magazine he'd been reading and glanced out the open window at her. "Yes."

"What are you doing here? Are you following me?"

"How amusing, Miss Wallace. You flatter yourself."

"I guess so."

He shrugged. "Hunters Heights is a small town. Do you not often run into people whom you know?"

It was her turn to shrug. She *was* being hard on him, and she didn't understand why. Some welcome to this country.

"I really am sorry about yesterday." She smiled at Jessie. "This gentleman—Mr. Marek is his name—and I had a bit of a minor traffic accident yesterday."

Jessie's eyes widened. "Are you all right?"

It was the first time she had spoken since running out of the doctor's office. She seemed perfectly all right now, Wendy thought. No trace of the pale child from inside.

"Just a bit bruised in spirit, that's all. I'm usually not this rude—believe me. Let me make it up to you in a small way, Mr. Marek. Let me buy you a cup of coffee, all right?"

He considered for a moment, then nodded. "Very well. Where?"

She considered for a moment. "Do you know the Olympian Diner just down the road on the right? How about going there?"

He nodded. "Excellent. Then I will see you in a few minutes?"

"All right. I have to make a phone call anyway. Come on, Jessie."

In the past few minutes she had remembered that she needed to call the school and tell them that Jessie wouldn't be in today. She couldn't pretend that she was Jessie's mother, so she'd just strip the story to its bare bones and say she was a neighbor watching Jessie today. And that appeared to be the case anyway. She would let Jessie's mom and the school sort things out tomorrow.

As they got into the car, Wendy realized Marek had never answered her, had never said why he was in the parking lot, sitting in a car. Maybe he was waiting for one of his relatives.

Maybe.

*     *     *

Dr. Thorne watched from his office window as the small brown car with the woman and child pulled out of the parking lot. Then a few minutes later the other car, the dark blue one, did the same.

He had seen the blue car several times over the past weekend. But then he noticed quite a bit.

He watched until he could see them no longer, then he turned around and sat at his desk.

The child, Jessie, had acted quite strangely. He wondered if it were some sort of hysterical reaction. Why? He had never had a patient react as she did. If he had, he wouldn't be receiving the humanitarian award this Saturday, he thought wryly.

Still, some children were shy or frightened when they came to the doctor . . . much the same way a pet responds to the vet. Everyone expected a painful shot. Little girls were often the worst, he reflected, and had to be gently coaxed. Yes, he had seen that behavior often enough. But not this time.

The look in her eyes . . . the expression on her face . . .

Her reaction brought back memories he thought long buried.

He had seen that haunted look before.

A long, long time ago.

He had seen that look on the faces of other children . . . of little boys, and most particularly of pretty little girls.

# ELEVEN

The Olympian Diner looked pretty much like any other diner in the state of New Jersey, Wendy decided. Reflective silver on the outside and shaped like the railroad cars that diners really used to be in the old days; inside, a long counter with stools and booths—always a fake red leather, too—up against the bank of windows. Not overly skillful oils and watercolors by local artists adorned the walls, and over the pass-through counter to the kitchen was a black clock shaped like a cat; the tail was a pendulum, and the eyes moved back and forth with each flick of the tail.

She and Jessie had seated themselves in a booth at the front, Jessie next to the window. Wendy was a regular here, and the waitresses knew her fairly well. The diner was open twenty-four hours a day, and sometimes Wendy liked to get out of the house late at night when everything else local had closed up. She would come here with a paperback to read or a notebook to scribble in, drink coffee, and watch the lights of the cars sweeping along the road. The food wasn't bad, either; it wasn't precisely a four-star place, but the dishes were always hearty and tasty. What more could you want from a restaurant? she asked herself. Besides inexpensive food, that is.

The waitress, a short blond with bright polish on her long nails and a stain on the skirt of her white uniform, brought them glasses of water and red menus so huge that Jessie could barely hold hers.

"Hungry?" Wendy asked as she watched the girl look down the lengthy list of items.

Jessie nodded.

"Then order whatever you want," Wendy said.

Jessie glanced up at that. "Really?"

"Really."

[ 65 ]

She hadn't had breakfast this morning. She'd been about to make it when Jessie came by. Normally Wendy didn't get up this early, but she had work to do and on days like that she couldn't sleep in, no matter how late she had stayed up the night before. Sister Rosalie and Sister Mary Michael had been insistent that she get up and attend to their business today. Of course, now it seemed like she wasn't going to get much work done. But that was okay. Jessie was a good kid, and Wendy liked her. Yet something, Wendy knew, was wrong.

She wanted to talk, but this wasn't the place. Maybe later when they went home.

The waitress came back for their order.

"We're waiting for someone, and would like to order when he gets here."

"Okay. I'll bring some coffee, okay?"

"Fine."

A minute or so later Wendy saw Marek's car drive up. He parked a few rows behind her own.

He saw them when he entered, and headed back to their booth. From where he sat across from them he could look out the window and see the Thorne Clinic, barely a quarter of a mile away.

Wendy signaled the waitress for another cup of coffee.

"I hope that's what you want, after all."

"Of course. May I be permitted a Danish or some such pastry? I did not have my breakfast this morning."

"That makes all of us," Wendy said.

They occupied themselves with studying the menus for a few minutes longer. Wendy had thought Jessie would want something like a cheeseburger, but the girl ordered a more sensible meal of blueberry pancakes. Marek would get his Danish, and she'd have some toast. That was about as much food as she could face before noon.

Jessie was busy drawing on the paper place mat with a pen Wendy had handed to her.

"And what were you doing at the doctor's, young lady?" Marek asked Jessie as he set his coffee cup down. He watched her sketch along the white border of the place mat.

She glanced up and shrugged in the offhanded way kids have. "I wasn't feeling good."

"This is your daughter?" he asked Wendy.

Wendy shook her head. "Nope, she's a new neighbor." She introduced the two, then said, "Jessie's mother is indisposed today."

"I'm sorry to hear that, Jessie."

"Um," the girl said as she put down her pen and poured syrup across her pancakes, making an intricate pattern with the sticky liquid. "She's always getting headaches. I should be used to it by now, you know."

"I see." Marek glanced across at Wendy who just shook her head.

The girl had been quite talkative since Marek arrived. Quite a contrast to the pale trembling child in the doctor's office. Could Jessie suffer from some sort of seizure? Epilepsy, perhaps? If she did, the girl would doubtless say nothing; she'd probably be embarrassed.

"Which doctor did you see?" Marek said, as he deftly sliced through his Danish with a fork. He was studying his pastry, but Wendy really thought he was watching Jessie carefully.

"That man," she said through a mouthful of pancakes.

"Dr. Thorne," Wendy supplied.

"Ah." Marek cut another piece from his pastry. "I've heard good things about him."

"Well, I have a doctor, of course, but he doesn't take kids, so I needed someone to take Jessie to. I keep seeing this guy's name all over the newspapers and thought he'd be a good one to choose." For a moment she thought she saw Marek's face tighten, but it was probably a trick of the light or something; now he was smiling.

"What did he say? What illness do you have?"

"It's just a mild bug going around," Wendy said before Jessie could answer. "He says she'll be all right after she rests today."

Jessie glanced up at her with a grateful expression and took a sip of her milk.

"That's good. You wouldn't want to get sick and miss your school. My nephew and niece go to the junior high here, you know."

"They have the same last name as you?" the girl asked. "Maybe they'll be in some of my classes." She seemed to brighten, almost as if she knew someone now.

"I'll tell them to introduce themselves."

"Okay."

The three chatted for a half hour or so, and finally Marek said he must go. He thanked Wendy for the coffee and Danish, and left. Jessie waved to him as he got into his car; he returned the wave.

Wendy watched as Marek pulled his car out of the parking lot and turned back in the direction of the clinic. Somehow, though, she knew this time he wouldn't be sitting in the parking lot.

For the first time she thought that Stefan Marek might well be a dangerous man.

Back at the house Jessie played with Dudley, while Wendy did her dinner dishes from the night before. She watched out of the corner of her eye as Jessie wrestled with the dog. The girl was exceedingly gentle with him. She knew that Jessie would love to run outside in the yard with Dudley—the stomachache and sore throat were long forgotten—but she also knew that Jessie feared her mother might see her.

Wendy sighed. What a sad way to live.

Finally, she finished and dried her hands on a towel, then stared down at Jessie, sitting cross-legged in the middle of the kitchen. She held onto one end of a long red rubber toy; the other end was clenched in Dudley's teeth, and his four paws were planted firmly on the tile as he mock-growled and tugged at the plaything.

Dogs and kids were a good combination, and she thought it was sad that Jessie's mother wouldn't let her have a pet. Obviously she craved one.

"Jessie."

"Yes, ma'am?"

These southern children, she thought. They're so polite. "Is anything wrong?"

Jessie blinked. "Wrong?"

"Yes. I was very worried about you this morning when you wouldn't answer the doctor's questions. You were trembling so badly, it was if you were freezing or something. I thought you might faint."

Jessie shrugged.

"Is there anything you want to talk about? An illness you might have had that hasn't gone away?" If the girl had epilepsy or something equally serious, she'd probably not want to come right out and admit it.

Jessie shook her head. "No, ma'am." She frowned slightly to herself, and Wendy thought she looked confused. Maybe Jessie didn't know why she had reacted the way she did.

"All right. If you ever want to talk, just remember my back door is open."

"Okay."

Wendy fed her lunch shortly after that and they talked about the movie *Jaws*, which was such a smash hit and had been held over at the theater for weeks now. Wendy had seen it twice already and really liked it, and Jessie wanted to go—except that her mother wouldn't let her; she said it was altogether inappropriate for children of tender years.

Jessie opened the back door with her key and paused, one foot across the threshold. She held her breath as she listened.

The house was just as silent as when she'd left that morning. She closed the door and tiptoed upstairs. A quick peek into the bedroom told her that her mother was still there. She saw her mom had been up at least once, though, because a half-filled glass sat on the nightstand within easy reach. Jessie knew that liquid wasn't water.

Medicine for her headaches, her mother claimed.

Jessie went into her room, closed the door, and lay down on the bed.

She didn't know what she would say when Patrick came home and asked her about her first day of school. She couldn't lie; they would find out real quick she hadn't been in school. She supposed she could tell the truth, but she wasn't sure he would believe her. If the school called tomorrow or tonight, she guessed Patrick would believe it. Would he yell because she'd missed the first day? What would her mother say? She guessed it was too late to worry about that.

Wendy had been nice to be so concerned about her and to take her to the doctor.

But that doctor—

She closed her eyes and the grayness enveloped her again. She felt hands clawing at her, elbows being thrust into her side, thumbs jabbed into her eyes as the strongest tried to get away; she could scarcely breathe there was so little air left and they were pushing pushing pushing toward the air that was left at the top of the black room, the air that was still all right, still breathable; she felt the bodies shoving, thrusting, shifting around her, felt the nude flesh in the darkness, heard the crying and praying and screaming, and she pushed out suddenly, but there was no way to get away from them, and then she slipped on something underfoot, something small that made a baby's wailing sound, and then she was falling and people were stepping on her and standing on her and she called out but no one heard in all the pandemonium and she felt a bone in her arm snap and—

Jessie blacked out.

# TWELVE

Sister Mary Michael was waiting for Sister Rosalie, Wendy typed.

Just as Marek had been waiting, she told herself. Or watching.

Or both, Wendy thought as she pushed back her desk chair and flipped off the light in her office. She wandered down to the bathroom, ran water in the sink, washed her face, and patted it dry. She changed into her short summer nightgown, brushed her teeth, drank a glass of water, ran a brush through her hair—why she did this before going to bed when she was just going to mess it up she didn't know, but it was a habit of long standing—and went into the bedroom. She didn't bother turning on a light; she didn't feel much like reading tonight.

The cats were already sacked out on the window seat where they could catch the cool night breezes, and Dudley lay on the bed, waiting for her. She patted him, then crawled under the sheet. The dog shifted so he could be closer to her.

Who was Marek waiting for and watching?

Someone at the Thorne clinic. Patient or doctor? Or nurse? she asked herself.

And why?

You're too damned nosy, Wallace. No one else would be bugged by this—only she would. So she'd keep turning it over and over in her mind until she figured out the puzzle.

If, indeed, there really was a puzzle. Maybe she just wanted there to be one because that was her profession, to write mysteries.

Maybe there was another reason she was interested in this.

Outside she could see a light in the distance—no doubt a streetlight on another avenue. She heard the faint sounds of traffic and the rustling of some night creature on the lawn, probably that hungry raccoon. Dudley raised his head, then decided it was too much of an effort to go and look. The cats didn't even look out, so it must have been nothing much to bother about.

That second reason.

Stefan Marek himself. He was a curious man. Very curious. In some ways he reminded her of Phil. Both dark and good-looking and somewhat on the formal side.

Phil. She shook her head. Why, she hadn't thought about him in—well—days, or was it hours? She'd like to think some day that might stretch out to months and maybe years. Maybe some day.

She tried not to think of her ex-husband, who would at that moment expound to her in that pedantic way of his that she was really making too much of nothing, and that Marek had every right to be where he was, doing what he was doing, whatever that was. You're just using that overactive imagination, he would say.

Overactive imagination. As if she were eight, and imagined she'd seen ghosts.

Which was one of the big problems for her and Phil. He had never understood that she really was a woman, that she wasn't a little girl who had to be completely protected. He hadn't wanted a wife; he'd wanted a daughter. Too bad they both hadn't figured that out before the wedding.

At least they hadn't been married a decade with a string of children; at least it had been a clean simple divorce. Very unmessy. At least it was done and over with and she was well rid of him.

But still . . .

Still, at times she missed him. Or rather, she supposed, she missed the company. There had been good times, of course, but fewer as the years passed. But sometimes, on nights like this, she missed the other body in the bed, a warmer and larger body than Dudley's.

She sighed audibly and the dog reached out and nuzzled her hand.

She closed her eyes, and saw Marek's face.

Go to sleep, she ordered. But she couldn't. All she could do was think about Stefan Marek and how good-looking he was and how curious. Quite interesting, she told herself. Very, very interesting.

A mystery, she told herself and smiled, because she was very good at puzzling out mysteries.

Stefan Marek sat in the hard-backed chair in his room at the Addison Bed-and-Breakfast and brought out his hard-sided suitcase from under the bed. It was an ugly gray-brown, the sort of baggage he knew Americans would presume all good Communists carried.

He had made sure his door was locked; he didn't want anyone accidentally bumbling into his room. He supposed most everyone in the establishment was already in bed. He didn't hear anyone moving about, and besides, it was well after midnight. He had learned that Mrs. Addison and her charges seemed to retire well before eleven. Fine with him. She had not been particularly talkative with him tonight at dinner.

He unlocked the suitcase and flipped it open.

The top concealed a secret compartment and now he opened that. Several objects were wrapped in plastic and cloth to keep them from harm in the long journey from Prague. They were hard to smuggle into the country now; customs and airport security had grown tighter with all the recent airplane hijackings. Still, he had managed. He had done it on more than one occasion; doubtless he would do it again.

Karel had wanted him to buy in this country, but he had thought that too chancy. He was, after all, an alien. And one from a Communist country. Certainly Karel had contacts after all these years in the States, but even so, he had preferred to bring his own.

Marek liked to be prepared well ahead of time—and to rely on no one but himself. He'd had that lesson instilled into him long ago. Plus he liked to use a weapon he was accustomed to. There was a certain feel to something his hand was accustomed to holding.

The room was warm—he had pulled the curtains shut, so that no one could see into the room either by accident or design—and he'd rolled up his sleeves.

He glanced down at the line of numbers tattooed on his left forearm. He moved his arm in the light and thought how little faded was the tattoo after thirty-three years.

But then it was indelible ink, made to last a lifetime, however short or long that might be.

He took out the larger bundle and carefully unwrapped it. The 9 mm Brno pistol gleamed blue in the light of the one lamp. A gun made in the old country, he thought wryly—a good ol' Communist weapon.

He had used rifles before, but they were bulkier and harder to smuggle across borders. They were a long-distance weapon, too. He preferred something that could be used at a much closer range, something more—personal.

[ 73 ]

Carefully he stripped down the automatic and cleaned and oiled each piece carefully. He did not like using dirty weapons. They must be spotless. Slowly he assembled the 9 mm again, checked the fifteen-shot magazine, and wrapped it once more in the plastic. Then he checked his rounds.

Fifty bullets.

More than enough to kill a man.

# TUESDAY

# THIRTEEN

Thorne watched as the girl carefully checked the front door to make sure it was locked, then walked down Clark Street in the direction of her school. He knew where the junior high was; it wasn't hard to find, even though he had never been there before. After all, Hunters Heights was relatively small. He'd had hundreds of patients over the years who attended the place.

He noted that the child didn't move very fast, not as if she wanted to get there very quickly. He glanced at the clock on his dashboard. She had a good twenty minutes before the first bell rang; she could make it easily if she hurried.

The girl's house had been easy to locate. The neighbor had written the address on the form, of course, and all he had to do then was take a look at a local map. He glanced at the neighbor's house; no one was stirring there. Good. He had seen a cat sitting in one of the windows, and that was all.

The girl had reached the corner and was turning onto Franklin Road. Thorne started the Mercedes and a moment later slipped it into gear and followed at a sedate pace. The radio was on, but down low, tuned in to a New York City classical station, and he recognized the first lilting notes of Beethoven's *Pastoral* Symphony. He hummed along, occasionally marking time, his fingers tapping on the rim of the wheel.

He kept back, never getting too close nor too far away, and once he pulled over to the curb, as if he were searching for a particular house number. He didn't want the girl to know she was being followed, although she seemed almost oblivious to her surroundings.

He turned the radio up, so he could enjoy the music even more.

He stopped well enough away from the school grounds so that

no one there would get suspicious, and watched as she walked through the gates of the school and down the long sidewalk. She didn't look around as she headed for the main building.

You could always tell a school, he observed to himself, it was usually one of the ugliest buildings in a town. He wondered why architects designed places of learning to be so prisonlike.

He wondered if her stomach troubled her today. Would she be pale and trembling inside her classrooms? Or was she completely recovered?

A curious child. There was something that set her apart from all the others, and he decided he would have to get to know her better.

Jessie hugged her books closer to her chest and glanced around surreptitiously just before she entered her junior high school. She'd had the creepiest feeling all morning that she was being watched, but when she looked around she couldn't see anyone. She hadn't made a big deal of it, though; if someone was watching her, she certainly didn't want them to know she knew.

She yawned. She was tired, even though she had slept all last night. In fact, she had slept through dinner and through the night and had only awakened just before her alarm was due to go off.

She had dressed quickly and carefully in the clothes she had intended to wear yesterday, eaten a piece of plain bread for breakfast, and glanced into her mother's room to see that she was once more not getting up. Today, though, Jessie knew she had to go to school. There was a tiny knot in her stomach, but nothing like it had been yesterday, which was good.

There was no note from Patrick, and she wondered why he didn't wake her for dinner. Maybe he had thought she was exhausted.

She had been; she still was. She tried not to yawn again. She'd had that strange nightmare again, and then nothing. She couldn't recall a single thing.

Jessie took a deep breath and hurried inside.

She went to the office and explained she had been sick the day before, and the people in administration gave her a slip of paper that told her the classes she would have, and the names of her teachers. She barely glanced at it; she would examine it later. The first bell was going to ring within minutes.

She left the office and followed a group of chattering students heading toward her first classroom. The teacher was already there. She gave the woman her name, and she pointed to the chair in the back that was Jessie's. Good, she wouldn't have to sit in the front; she always hated that. You couldn't daydream that way, and the teachers always liked to call on the ones who sat toward the front. Maybe back here she wouldn't be noticed.

She slid into her desk just as the first bell of the day rang. With a yawn Jessie flipped open her loose-leaf notebook.

English and math and science and history. The same old stuff, Jessie thought by lunchtime, feeling relieved that everything was more familiar than she had expected it to be. She was on the second lunch shift, which came at noon. She was glad she didn't have to eat any earlier. She hadn't packed anything for lunch, but she had remembered to stick some money in a pocket so she could buy something.

She filed through the cafeteria line and found a nearly deserted table. She began poking at the macaroni and cheese with her fork. She didn't talk to anyone, even though she saw some kids that were in some of her classes. She wondered if Mr. Marek's niece and nephew were in the lunchroom. She glanced around, but didn't see anyone resembling him. She thought she saw someone she'd seen at her birthday party, someone who lived on Clark Street, but she couldn't be sure.

Her first day back at school hadn't been so bad, she decided, as she opened her carton of milk. So far no one had made fun of her accent. That had surprised her. In history her teacher had asked her to stand and talk for a few minutes about where she had come from, and the other kids had actually seemed interested. Maybe this school wouldn't be so bad, after all. This afternoon she had PE, study hall, geography, and her advanced art class; she was looking forward to that.

The windows of the cafeteria faced the front of the school, and she could see most of Foster Street from where she sat. A silver car went by slowly, and she frowned. She thought she had seen that vehicle before. She speared a macaroni with her fork and ate it.

Yeah, she had seen it. On the way to school this morning. She had spotted the silver car—a Mercedes—parked a few houses up from her house. She knew it was a Mercedes, because Patrick had once pointed one out to her, saying it was the finest car around and that maybe he would someday have one.

[ 79 ]

Then she had seen the Mercedes drive along Foster during her first class.

And here it was again.

Maybe the driver lived on this street, and the woman or man behind the wheel had a lot of errands to run.

Why would it have been on her street? Maybe it wasn't the same car.

Maybe it was just a coincidence.

She stared out the window at Foster Street and the silver Mercedes drove by again. Gradually things around her began turning gray, and the noise in the cafeteria receded. Not here! she cried silently. She shook her head, violently, again and again, as if that swift motion would somehow dispel the sounds and the feelings, and pressed her fingernails into the palms of her hand. The pain shot through her, and somehow brought her back. Gradually the clamor of the lunchroom—the shrill voices, the scraping of metal chairs, music from a radio in the kitchen—returned to her.

She finished the last of her lunch and headed back to her locker with minutes to spare before her next class.

PE was, well, physical education, and you really couldn't say much about it, Jessie decided; either you liked it or you didn't. Mostly she liked it. Luckily the teacher and her fellow students didn't do anything but talk today; in the next few days they would be starting soccer. Next in her schedule came the advanced art class. She knew she would enjoy this the most of all; it was challenging but fun.

Things slowed down in geography, her next-to-last period, and she began to feel even more tired than she had when she got up that morning. She yawned and tried to pay attention to the teacher, but he had such a droning voice that it was hard to care that they needed to learn the capitals of the South American countries by the end of the week.

This time her assigned seat was in the row alongside the windows. She yawned, jotted something down, and looked out the window.

A silver car passed along the street.

She blinked, and as if from a distance she heard a strange churning noise, a sound like the wheels of a train rattling down a rail, and then she heard the shrill whistle, and then came that terrible sickeningly sweet smell, the smell that closed her throat, that cloyed around her, that seemed to stain her very skin and hair, that made her want to gag, made her want to throw up.

She gasped and slapped a hand across her mouth and ran from the room and down the hall to the girls' bathroom. She made it just in time. She knelt by one of the toilets and threw up until there was nothing left in her stomach, not a single bit of macaroni.

"Jessica?" she heard a woman's voice. It was one of her teachers. "Are you all right?"

She wiped her mouth off with some toilet paper and flushed everything. Taking a deep breath, she came out of the stall and saw Mrs. Cordero standing by the sinks and looking really worried.

"I guess I don't feel as good as I thought I did earlier, ma'am," Jessie said. She walked over to a sink, cupped her hands and drank some of the water, rinsed her mouth, then spat it back into the sink. She ran the water for a long time, then washed her hands. She was trembling, but didn't want her teacher to see that. When she glanced in the mirror over the sink, in the harsh bathroom light she thought she looked as pale as if she'd seen a ghost.

"Do you want to go home? Do you want me to call your mother?"

"No, ma'am, please don't call my mother. She hasn't been feeling well, either," Jessie said quickly. "School's almost over for the day; I've just got study hall next. I'll go home now and take it real easy tonight. I think I'll be okay. Maybe it's first day nerves, ma'am." She smiled tentatively.

Mrs. Cordero, who seemed like a really nice person for a teacher, smiled reassuringly. "I bet it is. You've come a long way, and New Jersey isn't much like Kentucky. There's a lot of settling in for you."

Jessie nodded.

"If you want to sit in the nurse's office for a while, I'll take you down there."

"No, that's okay, ma'am. I'll come back to class. Thank you, Mrs. Cordero."

The woman smiled at her again.

Jessie paused to drink at the water fountain and then followed Mrs. Cordero back to where Mr. Lee was still lecturing.

# FOURTEEN

At the end of the block, Stefan Marek watched from the corner of his eye as once more the silver Mercedes drove past him and then turned onto Pine, which ran across Foster. He shifted and gazed in the rearview mirror and waited for the car to circle back. It didn't.

It had passed by the junior high five times during the course of the day. Very curious. He had followed it here this morning from Clark Street and then he'd parked. He was very well prepared. In case anyone should ask, in case anyone should notice, he had his story ready; he was doing a series of articles on small-town America for his Prague newspaper. However, most people didn't notice parked cars and their occupants; most people were too much in a hurry to get where they were going. It worked to his advantage.

He started up the Buick and in leisurely fashion followed the silver Mercedes and its driver.

Why, he asked himself, would Dr. Thorne keeping going by the Hunters Heights Junior High? It was the school Marek's cousin's two children attended, and it was where that little girl he met yesterday went.

What business could bring Thorne there, particularly when he never got out of the car? It couldn't have anything to do with his practice, despite his no doubt having dozens of students at the school as patients.

Curious.

Maybe, Marek thought with a tightening of his lips, Thorne had an outside interest in children—an unhealthy interest.

He saw the Mercedes ahead, and allowed himself to drop back a car's length. He didn't want to get too close now. Thorne put on his signal and turned left, and Marek saw that the doctor was heading back to the clinic.

Good.

Marek had some reading to catch up on; while Thorne was in the clinic, he would have time.

Jessie left school before study hall and glanced around often while she walked home, but she didn't see anyone following her. Wendy was in her front yard and so she stopped to chat for a while and to pat Dudley, and then she went inside the house.

"Well, sugar, how was your day?" Astrid Fields smiled at her from where she had set up a bookcase and was filling it with books. The books—mostly large art books and biographies of famous artists—were those of Jessie's dad, and her mother had wanted to throw them out when they were getting ready to move, but Jessie wouldn't let her. Even Patrick had said she couldn't get rid of them because maybe the kid could use them for schoolwork, and so they had been packed, albeit reluctantly, by her mother.

Her mother hadn't noticed she was home early; good. "Hi, Mom. It was just fine." She would never say anything about her spells to her mother. Never. She headed for the refrigerator and took out an apple. Fruit was encouraged for snacks in her house, and luckily she liked apples and oranges and bananas. Still, she wouldn't say no to Wendy's cookies, if they should be offered again sometime.

"You like your teachers?"

"They seem okay." They were *teachers*. What did her mother expect?

"That's good, honey. Good teachers are somethin' to value, believe me." Astrid hesitated, then pushed on. "I got a call this mornin' from the school."

Jessie paused at the foot of the stairs. She didn't know what to expect.

Her mother's expression was slightly puzzled now. "The administration lady who called said that you weren't feelin' well yesterday and that the lady next door took you to the doctor. Is that so, Jessica Mae?" Jessie nodded. Astrid looked slightly hurt. "Now, honey, why ever didn't you let me know you weren't feelin' well? I could have taken you to the doctor, you know."

"I didn't want to bother you, Mom. I knew you were having a bad headache, and Miss Wallace is really nice and I just sort of went over there."

"You are such a sweet and thoughtful child, did you know that?

[ 83 ]

I guess I ought to go over and say thanks. It's nice to have good neighbors, isn't it, Jessica Mae?"

Jessie nodded as she went upstairs. Her mother didn't expect her to stay to talk, which was good; she wanted to be by herself. She paused at the landing, her hand on the banister. "I'm going to do my homework now, Mom."

"All right, honey, but remember to wash your hands before supper." Jessie rolled her eyes. Her mother *always* said that—as if Jessie could somehow forget. "Your dad will be home around seven or so."

"Stepfather," Jessie said softly. She went into the guest bedroom that faced the street and looked out the window. No sign of anything unusual. Good.

Jessie hurried into her bedroom. She shut the door, making sure she didn't slam it. That would bring her mother upstairs and her mother would want to know why she was acting like such a tomboy slamming doors and such, and Jessie really didn't want to talk to her, not now.

She dumped her books on her desk and crossed over to sit on the bed. She picked up one of her stuffed animals and hugged it tight, wishing not for the first time that it was a real animal, warm and cuddly.

She realized she'd been holding her breath and with effort she inhaled. She was safe, she told herself.

Safe.

At least for a while.

# FIFTEEN

Wendy finished the last of her turkey sandwich and pushed away the plate so she could put her notebook back on the table. She always removed it while she ate, on the off chance that she might knock her cup of coffee or glass of water over on the paper. She read during dinner; that was safe.

Now, though, she needed to make some notes. She had come here after six for dinner and had decided to just stay and continue working.

She signaled the waitress that she'd like another cup of coffee, opened the spiral-bound notebook to the page where she'd already jotted down some lines, then tapped her pen against her lips. Across the diner she heard the door open, then close with a squeak. This was a busy time of the night for the diner. Often she watched who came and who went, but right now she had to concentrate. She had figuratively painted Sister Rosalie into a corner, and she wasn't sure how to tie everything together, much less get the other nun into it.

She was aware of Edie, the regular waitress on this shift, filling her cup again and moving off. The woman would freshen up the coffee several times without having to ask and would come back in about an hour to see if she wanted some dessert. At least that was the ritual they'd established so far.

Wendy reached for her cup, sipped the coffee, and set it down, all without looking up.

She heard the door open and close again; once more she paid little attention, until she sensed someone watching her.

She glanced up. In the booth across from her sat Dr. Thorne, a newspaper unfolded before him. She smiled at him, not sure that he would recognize her. Although she had just seen him yesterday, he was sure to have had lots of people come through his office already since then.

He stared at her for what seemed a long time, then smiled. "Ah, Miss Wallace, how are you? How is the little girl today?"

"Jessie's doing much better. She returned to school today."

"Well, if she begins to feel badly again, then I suggest that she stay home. I think she is just unsettled because of the move. It's tough on a child of her years, and this is a different climate, as well."

She nodded. "Thanks." She saw that he hadn't ordered yet and didn't seem to be waiting for anyone, and she decided to get a little bold. "Would you care to join me?"

"I don't want to bother you," he said, a trifle hesitantly.

"It's no bother. Really."

"That would be very nice, thank you." He folded his newspaper precisely, slid out of the booth, and came over to hers. He had no sooner sat across from her than the waitress showed up with the menu. "Thank you," he murmured politely. "You have already eaten, I see." He nodded to her empty platter.

"Yes, but I plan on having dessert."

"Good."

"You look very much at home here," Dr. Thorne said after he had ordered, nodding to the notebook and her paperback and the several pens scattered across the tabletop.

"Sometimes I like to work here. I work out of my house and I really don't get out much, so it's nice to come to the diner and just sit and have some coffee and watch other folks or eat dinner."

"What do you do in your house?" He watched her carefully.

Ah, the two-dollar question, with the two-dollar answer that always got her such odd reactions: puzzled stares, blank looks, and rarely, ever so rarely, genuine interest.

"I'm a novelist."

"I see. What kind?"

"Mystery, although I've done some others."

"Wallace. Hmmmm." He tapped his fingers briefly on the tabletop, as if in beat to some silent music. "You have a series out, is that not correct? Sister Rosalie and Sister Mary Michael?"

Wendy gave him a look of astonishment. "You've heard of my books?"

"Not only have I heard of them, but I've read them and enjoyed them immensely. I thought your name was familiar yesterday when you brought Jessie in, so when I went home I caught sight of one of your books and I knew then why it was familiar."

"Amazing! I have to tell you, Dr. Thorne, that you're just about the first person in this town who's ever owned up to reading one of my books. Most everyone just looks at me as if I'd sprouted antennae. They can't seem to cope with someone who creates characters and situations every day."

"Most people don't have a streak of creativity or originality. Most people in our society act very much like automatons, responding to orders from above. They could not, if their lives depended upon it, create something from their minds."

She shrugged. "Probably so. I'm sure I'd get more attention if I were a plumber."

"Ah, a lady plumber . . . that would be quite unique, but not as amusing, I think, as writing. What does your husband think of your writing?"

Her smile faltered just a little. "I'm no longer married."

Immediately he looked embarrassed, as if he overstepped some boundary. "I'm sorry. I didn't mean to pry."

"You didn't. As for your question . . . well, before our divorce and before I sold anything, my husband was very supportive. When I made my first sale and then my second, he became less and less encouraging. I guess in some strange way he thought he was being threatened. I don't know why; he wasn't doing the same thing."

"The human mind is very odd; we can't always say why we react the way we do. We may try to rationalize something, and yet be reacting on some primitive level."

"No doubt. Ah, here's your dinner." She ordered dessert after Edie put Thorne's dishes down, and then she reached for her cup of coffee. "Do you come in here often, Doctor?"

He nodded through a mouthful of beef. When he could, he spoke. "It's close to the clinic and fast, and sometimes I come here just to get out of the office and have a quick bite to eat, and then it's back to work again."

"You put in a lot of long days then?"

"Yes. Tonight is one. I have much paperwork to go through, and I prefer to do that in the evenings when things are quiet and I'm by myself."

"I meant to ask you something yesterday, although there really wasn't time. I thought I heard a slight accent in your voice. Where are you from originally?"

"Switzerland," he replied. "I lived in a small town just outside Geneva."

They chatted about his life in Switzerland and various other things. Wendy learned that the pediatrician was quite well read. Mysteries and thrillers were his favorite novels, he declared, although he liked a good science fiction now and then too. They talked about some of the recent movies they'd seen, and the *Jaws* phenomenon. Finally, some two hours later, he looked at his watch and said he should be getting back to the office.

"I enjoyed our chat. Perhaps we can do it again, Miss Wallace," Thorne said.

She nodded. She didn't think she would mind that. He was an interesting man—and attractive, too, one part of her insisted.

"Of course. I'll probably be here," she said airily. "Taking notes."

"Good luck with your nuns," he said, inclined his head slightly and walked away.

Dr. Thorne paid at the cash register, chatted with the hostess there, and left a moment later, and Wendy went back to work. A number of cups of coffee later she got up to leave, and discovered that Thorne had paid for her meal as well.

She was surprised, but not displeased. He was European and old-fashioned, no doubt, and it wasn't such a bad thing to have your meals paid for once in a while. As a simple courtesy, she told herself.

Funny, she thought as she got into the Rabbit, that she should have met two European men in such a short time. What a difference there was between them.

Night and day. Absolute night and day.


Marek sat inside his car in the parking lot of the Olympian Diner and watched as first Thorne left, and then, nearly an hour later, Wendy Wallace.

He had followed Thorne back to the clinic, then realized the doctor would be working there for hours, so he returned to the diner parking lot to sit and wait and to see what he could see.

He had been astounded to see the two of them talking. How did they know one another? Ah yes, yesterday the woman had mentioned taking the girl to a doctor. This must be the one. Or it was conceivable that Wendy Wallace knew the doctor from some other place. This was, after all, not a very large town, and people tended to meet each other more frequently.

Was it a chance meeting? Or prearranged? Thorne had not sat immediately with her, but had only gone over to her booth after a few minutes.

What could they have been talking about?

Marek still didn't understand how they had come to be at the diner together. Surely, it was just a chance meeting, although he couldn't dismiss the alternative.

He yawned and glanced at his watch, which he could just make out by the light from the street. After eight-fifteen. He was tired and hungry and had to take a leak; he hadn't had his dinner yet because he had been too busy watching Thorne and then Wendy Wallace.

Now it was time for his meal. He didn't think he would have any more work to do tonight.

Marek got out of the car and headed for the diner door. They were having a particularly good business tonight, he thought ironically.

A middle-aged waitress whose nametag read "Edie" seated him in the very booth that Thorne and Wendy had been in earlier, and he glanced around to see if either had left anything by accident. Nothing.

He ordered a full meal. While he waited he looked out into the darkness, and decided that there seemed more to this situation than he'd first suspected.

Maybe he ought to get to know the woman better. She might be a key to this.

And he couldn't afford not to know.

# SIXTEEN

Jessie sat at her desk, with only the student lamp on the desk lit, and took out an eight-by-eleven pad of white drawing paper.

Carefully she folded the cover back and selected a pencil from her metal box. A hard lead—#3 or maybe #2½—to begin with, she decided. Her father had always told her to start light, then move to the darker leads. You couldn't erase a heavy black streak, he had told her many times. She tapped the eraser end of the pencil against the pad.

Now what to draw? Her dad always said the best thing to do was picture what you wanted to sketch in your mind. He said it was just like watching TV or a movie, only you controlled what happened.

She closed her eyes and concentrated hard. What did she see?

She scratched her nose with the eraser, squinted at the light, closed her eyes again. And saw—

A high barbed-wire fence, and a train track not far from it, and beyond that bleak ugly buildings darkened now at night, and—

Suddenly the door to her room flew open. Jessie dropped the pencil and opened her eyes. She looked at the doorway, startled, and for some reason more than a little afraid.

It was Patrick.

And he wasn't smiling. The light from the hallway made almost a halo around him, and he seemed bigger than he really was. Threatening, too. She picked up the pencil and gripped it hard, trying not to let her hand shake.

"Your mother says you haven't bathed since Saturday."

"I have," she said.

"Are you saying that your mother is a liar?"

A trap. No matter what she said, it didn't matter. She just shook her head. She could try to tell him that she had bathed, using a washcloth again and letting the sink fill up with hot water and lots of soap. But she didn't think he cared. He hadn't liked her explanation the first time she gave it.

"Come on," Patrick said, his voice not unkind now.

She set the pencil down by the drawing paper, got her night T-shirt and a change of panties, and followed her stepfather into the bathroom.

Patrick hadn't spoken to her much since he had gotten home about an hour ago; he hadn't said much to her mother, either. Mostly he had sat at the table, shoveled in his dinner, and grunted when either one had asked him something. She didn't think his new job was going very well; her mom had asked a few questions about it, then stopped when he didn't answer. She didn't think that boded very well for either her or her mother. So right after dinner she had come upstairs to work on her homework and then her drawing. She wanted to stay out of everyone's way.

Without a word he wrenched the spigots on and within minutes the shower stall began filling with steam. He towered in front of her and jerked his thumb to the left toward the stall.

. . . to the left . . . the left . . . she did not want to go to the left.

The intense light glared in her eyes, hurting them because she had been so long in the darkness, and she was so hungry, so thirsty from the days without food or water. She tried to lick her lips with her swollen tongue, but couldn't; she could feel her lips cracked and bleeding and she sucked greedily at the moisture. Beyond a high wire fence flames, yellow and orange, so hellish, belched upward, and there was the stench that had enveloped her the minute she had stepped out of the train. Bits of ash settled on her face and she brushed away the soot, greasy beneath her fingers. Immediately she wiped her hand down the side of her coat. Somewhere dogs barked, unfriendly animals, dogs that would tear her to pieces in a moment, she knew, rather than lick her hand, and she heard men shouting roughly in an ugly language. Someone shoved her hard on her shoulder and she stumbled forward—her eyes wide open and unseeing—her clothes dropping from her hands—someone was yelling at her—yelling—screaming—and pushing her—pointing to the left— and she knew she didn't want to go to the left—she didn't —not to the left—the left meant she would die—and she didn't want to die, not now not now not now . . .

The stench receded and the barking dogs were gone and the

[ 91 ]

light faded, until it was only the gleam of a bathroom overhead fixture, there was the sound of Patrick's voice as he shouted at her.

He kept shouting at her, and she didn't know why. She couldn't understand him. Someone slapped her across the thigh, then the cheek. Her cheek stung from the impact, but she ignored it.

She looked at him, beyond him, and moved to the left, moved toward the shower.

Once more Jessie began screaming.

Home now for more than two hours, Dr. Thorne was relaxing as he gazed around his den. It was a comfortable room, one that looked lived in, and was spacious as well, much the largest in the house, with a couple of old leather couches and chairs, an old oriental rug with more than its share of stains on it, an immense wooden desk in one corner, a flagstone fireplace along one side of the room, and books and magazines everywhere. On the wall flanking the fireplace he had hung more of his awards, and photos. The colors of the room were dark, masculine, and his wife had long ago given up trying to decorate it to match the rest of the house. She had thrown up her hands in good-natured defeat.

He smiled at the thought. That had been a long time ago. Dorothy had been dead nearly a decade now, the victim of a car accident in which the other driver had combined alcohol and LSD. When the man had stumbled from his demolished car, empty beer cans had rolled out of the car. There had been nothing the man of medicine could do to save his wife. Nothing. All the years of training, and nothing could be done.

He sighed heavily and glanced at the small oval photo of Dorothy on the desk. Small and blond, she hardly looked the fifty years of age she'd been when she died. His gaze went to the photo next to hers. This was of a young man who bore a striking resemblance to Thorne. Raymond Thorne, his son, a graduate assistant at Princeton. He would be up for the ceremony on Saturday. Thorne was looking forward to seeing him. The boy—a "boy," he thought with amusement, who was in his mid-twenties now—hadn't been home in a month or more, and Thorne missed him. They spoke often on the phone, but it wasn't the same.

Thorne only wished that Dorothy could be there with him. He sighed again. She would have loved to see him being honored. She had been his cheering section, the one to always encourage him, even when he despaired. Always cheerful, always inspiring.

[ 92 ]

He dropped onto one of the couches and rubbed his left leg. It was stiff today. The weather, no doubt. A sign of approaching rain; the old wound had proved to be an accurate barometer before. Still, the rain was needed after the long, hot, dry summer they'd had.

He shifted and picked up the novel he had been reading and set down on the table by the couch last night before going to bed.

*Saving Grace*, by Wendy Wallace. Well, he hadn't quite finished this novel of hers—the first he'd ever seen—and he hadn't precisely found it or its companions in his house. He had been at the bookstore on his lunch hour the day before and had seen the novel in the section reserved for local authors. That's when he'd made the connection. So out of curiosity he'd bought it, and a second one.

It wasn't bad, and somehow he was surprised. She didn't seem the type to write intricate mysteries. He wasn't sure what he expected from her. Actually, he couldn't know, could he? He hadn't talked with her all that long, although their dinnertime conversation had proved enjoyable.

She was an intelligent woman with a good sense of humor, he was surprised to find. He wasn't sure what he had expected. But not this. He had actually thought he would like to see the woman again.

If he saw Wendy Wallace on another occasion, he might also see her young neighbor.

Thorne's eyes narrowed and he stared at a distant spot on the opposite wall.

Young Jessie Morrison and the look she had worn yesterday—

He was familiar with that expression. Oh yes. He had seen it before. Too many times before.

He had seen the same expression on the faces of the two young girls in Buenos Aires in 1956; and in the eyes of the man in Zurich in '61, and in those of a woman in '67 when he had come through JFK on his way home from a ten-day-long medical conference in London. Recognition, horror, accusation—but in one so young it didn't make sense.

He knew, as he rubbed a hand over his face, that it wasn't over. *Yet how could she know?*

Outside in the darkness Stefan Marek watched as the light in the downstairs den window blinked out. One went on upstairs; after a few minutes that, too, was switched off.

He flicked his cigarette to the ground, stamped it out, then picked up the stub and methodically shredded the paper, spread the flakes of tobacco, and stuck the filter into his shirt pocket.

He smiled when he saw what he was doing. Old habits die hard.

He waited for a few minutes more to see if another light went on, but the house remained dark. It appeared that the doctor was done for the night.

End of the day for him as well.

All too soon tomorrow would be here.

The doctor pulled away from his position alongside the window and rubbed a knee that had become stiff from being immobile so long. The watcher had finally left, no doubt walking down to his car parked some distance away—the blue Buick he had seen on numerous occasions. It had taken a while tonight for the man to be persuaded that Thorne had gone to sleep.

He did not need to follow the watcher. He knew where the man would go now; he had been to the Addison Bed-and-Breakfast. He had discovered that a man from the old country—a *Jew*, the gossipy old bag of an owner had confided to him, and how shocked she was because he had seemed like such a *nice* man—was staying there. And he knew this man followed him.

That didn't bother Thorne, though. Jews had followed him before through the years. No doubt they would continue to follow him. It didn't matter. They didn't matter.

He had taken care of all the others; he would take care of this one as well.

Thorne smiled in the darkness.

# WEDNESDAY

# SEVENTEEN

"Ah, you again."

Wendy glanced up from the meat display, where she was about to reach for a packet of hamburger at only 99¢ a pound—she had decided she should stock up her freezer with it—to see one of the men she had just been thinking about the previous night. Stefan Marek stood there, a shopping cart in front of him.

"I hope we're not going to have an accident with these," she said with a wry smile as she tossed a four-pound pack of meat into her cart. Chicken breasts and a very small smoked ham followed.

"I trust not, especially since I have no insurance for this cart."

She chuckled and glanced over the contents of the man's basket; beneath the paper napkins and towels, she saw jars of pickles and olives and peppers, frozen vegetables and some bags of fresh veggies and fruit, several loaves of bread, and two large roasting chickens. "It looks like you're filling up for a siege."

He nodded solemnly. "It's for my aunt, actually. She's having a dinner tomorrow night, and I offered to go to the store for her. She works with my uncle at the glassworks and doesn't have a lot of free time. I, on the other hand, have much."

She wondered what he did with his time. Did he work here? For his uncle, perhaps? Or was he on vacation? On vacation in Hunters Heights? she asked herself. C'mon, Wendy. Still, he might just be visiting his family. Even then he would have to take some time off from that. For Pete's sake, look at her. She took time off from her books. He could do the same, couldn't he? Cut him some slack.

He's here to get some food for his aunt to save her the trouble the next day. How nice, how considerate . . . how false that struck her somehow.

Maybe she just wasn't used to men offering to do anything for women, anything that would save them trouble or time. God knows, Phil would never have been caught dead in a supermarket. Even if she'd run out of something while she was cooking, he would never go and get the item for her, no matter if he wasn't doing anything else.

There might actually be men who thought of others' feelings, she told herself.

It was hard for her to believe. And she realized how cynical she'd become over the past year.

Marek looked at the hamburger and the bags of hamburger rolls. "Are you planning a cookout?"

"Sure looks like it, doesn't it? I decided to stock up on stuff. That way I won't have to keep buying it when I come back." She shifted slightly, not sure what to say now. They seemed to have exhausted the food discussion.

"Look, Miss Wallace, I still feel bad about our accident. Perhaps we could have lunch together today? If you are not particularly busy?" He smiled, and she noticed the fine lines around his eyes. She thought he was older than he actually looked, or perhaps he had just had a hard life.

She hesitated, then asked herself, Why not? "Lunch would be fine, Mr. Marek, although I have to get this shopping done first, and run a few more errands after that."

"I know. Faye would be unhappy with me if I don't get this done after making such a fuss about volunteering. So, why don't we meet someplace in, say, an hour and a half or so?"

"Great."

"Any suggestions?"

"Yes, there's a steak house out on Old Mine Road, the Iron Forge. It's pretty nice, not too busy at this time of day, with good food and reasonable prices." She didn't know what he did for a living, and didn't know if he could afford a good restaurant. The Iron Forge wouldn't strain anyone's wallet.

"I know of it."

"Well, until then, Mr. Marek." She raised her hand in a slight wave and pushed her cart down the aisle where the pet food was located.

So, he still felt bad, did he? It was nice that he said that, even though she didn't believe it for a moment. She had to admit she was curious about him, and even more curious why he was seeking her out. Nonsense. Just because she'd met up with him twice now didn't mean he was seeking her out, did it?

Did it?

She finished her shopping—she looked around but didn't see Marek in any of the checkout lines; perhaps he'd already left—and then went home and unloaded everything. Dudley snuffled at her feet and generally complained about the lack of food in his dish, which she rectified. The cats followed her from room to room and meowed piteously until she finally stroked them.

She glanced at her watch and saw she had plenty of time. She took a quick shower, changed into a simple blouse and good jeans, and hurried out to the car. She checked her hair in the rearview mirror and wished she'd had time to use the curling iron. She didn't know why she was taking such care with her appearance. It wasn't like she was going on a date.

Right.

Marek's rental car was already in the parking lot when she drove up to the Iron Forge. She found him at a back table, well away from any window, and somehow that surprised her. He had struck her as the type who always had to be by a window so he could watch. At least he had been that way yesterday.

But watch for what? she wondered.

"Hi," she said, as she slid into the booth opposite him. "I hope I'm not too late."

"Not at all."

A moment later the waitress, dressed like the others in a modified Colonial costume, complete with white bonnet and apron, brought them menus. Wendy had been here several times—once with Phil, who had insisted they had been overcharged for inferior meat and badly cooked vegetables and had been loud and obnoxious about it. It had been a long time before she felt she could come back to the steakhouse.

"You're looking very thoughtful," Marek said.

She closed the menu. "Sorry."

"There is no need to be sorry, Miss Wallace."

"Wendy, please."

"Stefan, then."

They ordered and she asked him how long he had been in the country.

"A month now."

"Do you plan to stay much longer?"

He shrugged. "To be truthful, I don't know. I have some work to do here first, and I'm not sure how long that will take, and then I'll head back home."

"What do you do precisely?"

"I'm a journalist."

Her face lit up. "Really? I used to be one."

They spent some time discussing his plans on covering the bicentennial celebration and their journalistic experiences, although she knew her tiny newspaper was hardly in the same league as his. He had traveled throughout Europe to cover stories for his newspaper, while the farthest she'd been sent for hers was to Philadelphia, to report on a stamp exhibition.

It was warm inside the steakhouse, and Marek had already finished his second soda and, somewhere along the way, pushed up his sleeves. She caught sight of the tattoo and looked down at her plate.

He noted her reaction. "I'll put my sleeve down, if it bothers you."

Wendy looked up at him. "No, please. I'm sorry. That was rude of me. I shouldn't have looked away, but I was just taken aback."

He grinned, but it wasn't a pleasant expression. "Most of us don't flaunt it, I suppose."

"I don't know what to say."

"I don't suppose you could have known many survivors, particularly in a small town like this. Maybe if you were in New York City, or down in Florida." He shrugged. "Well, there aren't that many now. Not many came out of the camps, and over the years, they—we—have been dying off."

"You couldn't have been very old when you were there," she said. She thought he must be in his mid-forties, certainly no younger than that. "Look, Stefan, you don't have to talk about it, if you don't want. I certainly didn't mean to stir up old memories best forgotten."

He shook his head. "Best forgotten, perhaps, but not possible, I suspect. I really don't mind talking about it. As for how old I was . . . I was twelve, although I looked older than that, which was doubtless one of the things that saved me; and I was strong for my age, too; another good attribute." He cut his steak and speared a chunk with his fork.

She waited for him to go on; she didn't know what to say.

"I was living with my family in Prague when the Nazis invaded

[ 100 ]

it in '39. From that moment on we—that is, the Jews of Prague—were dismissed from our professions and our schools; our books and periodicals were banned; we couldn't use public transport, nor even outside telephones. Two years later in October my family and I were deported to the ghetto Theresienstadt, a so-called 'transit camp' outside of Prague, after everything we owned was appropriated by the Nazis. The next year we were shipped to Auschwitz. When we got there the Nazis made us form two lines. My father, my uncle, and I went to the right; my mother, my two brothers—younger than me by a number of years—my pregnant aunt, her three little girls, my grandfather, and my grandmother all went to the left and the gas chambers."

"I'm sorry." The words were inadequate for what she was feeling. She didn't know how to express it. Yet she felt he might know.

Marek shrugged. "It was a very long time. I am tempted to say that what's past is past, but I would be a liar if I did. It's something that I carry every day of my life, like an extra weight. I know there are those who have forced themselves to forget, but I never could. Before the invasion, there were seventy-two members of my family; after the war, there was my uncle and myself, who had survived the camp, and my other uncle— Karel—who had been away when we were sent east. Everyone else died, either in the ovens, through hard labor, or from disease; my own father died just a week before Auschwitz was liberated by the Russians." He signaled the waitress for another drink.

Wendy pushed her plate away; she couldn't eat any more. She took a sip of her soda, forcing herself to find the right words. "You stayed on in Prague when the camp was liberated?" She found that curious; she would have thought he would have wanted to get as far away as possible . . . to the U.S. or to Israel, perhaps.

"I had no other place to go. Prague was my home. Besides, I was never an ardent Zionist like so many others I knew, so Israel had no attraction for me; my family, you see, possessed Communist leanings—we were doubly 'blessed' then in the eyes of the Nazis for being both Jews *and* Communists. After the war I bounced around the countryside for a while, just trying to survive day-to-day. The camps may have been liberated and the detainees freed, but frankly, our own government didn't want us; it had its own momentous problems. No one wanted us. Only the Americans and British helped.

"Finally I made my way back home to what was left. I found my other uncle there and we started over. He was able to get his glassworks back—it had been converted to wartime use by the Nazis—and I worked with him for a while. Then I headed to England for more education; I returned later on and helped my uncle again. By then, he had decided to come over here and start a plant. He had already begun another family. I decided to stay in Czechoslovakia for a while, because by then it was Communist-ruled, and was this not the great salvation my family had waited for?"

Marek finished his soda and ordered another one, and asked her if she wanted more; she shook her head, and mentally raised an eyebrow at the line of glasses. A good thing, perhaps, that these weren't beers.

"You don't sound like a tried-and-true Communist, though. You sound more than a little disillusioned. That doesn't seem to be the proper party line, from what I know of Communists."

"Well, what works on paper doesn't always work when applied to real people and situations. We found ourselves going from one kind of tyranny to another, with much of the old prejudice in place."

"And it was after this then, that you became a journalist?"

"Yes, by then the glassworks held little interest for me—I was not cut out to be a pencil pusher—and I began working at one of the newspapers part time. That grew into a full-time job. And so here I am."

"Do you think you'd ever emigrate here?"

"I don't know. I like the U.S. very much; this is not my first visit, and I always enjoy myself when I'm here and wish I could come back more often and stay longer. However, you must understand, Czechoslovakia is home . . . despite everything."

She said nothing for a while, not sure what to speak of, and simply rattled the ice in her soda glass.

"What approach are you taking in your articles about the bicentennial?"

"Sort of an outsider's look at a most typical American celebration. There's some humor to it, and I hope to travel to other parts of the country to observe the celebration. Frankly, here in the East the bicentennial feeling is much more intense."

"This is where it all began."

"Yes." He signaled the waitress and, when she came over, ordered coffee for both of them. She declined dessert, while he decided to sample the blueberry pie. "Actually, I decided to do the articles because it had been some time since I'd seen my uncle and his family, and I thought I was due for a visit again. Of course, I will also do an article or two about the glassworks, although for one of the magazines."

"I would think there would be interest in this country about it, and about you as well."

"Perhaps."

Wendy studied the five soda glasses Marek had pushed to one side so the waitress could remove them.

"Simply disgusting, is it not? I confess that I have an incredible thirst, Wendy. I developed it in the camps—we were thirsty all the time—it was far worse, you know, than the hunger; that could be dealt with, but not the dehydration, which killed so many of us— and I decided a long time ago that I would never be thirsty again. Sometimes, I admit, it seems a bit ridiculous. Maybe one day I'll break the habit. I don't think I have to worry ever again about not having enough water to drink—but then again, you never know."

She nodded, not knowing what to say. She couldn't imagine going so long without something to drink that she became dehydrated, and she shuddered, thinking of what he must have suffered in the camp.

She studied Stefan Marek as he sipped his coffee, and thought how amazing was his story. And how utterly charming he was—and what an accomplished liar.

# EIGHTEEN

He had followed her to school again today, and again during the morning hours he had cruised up and down the street. Thorne didn't know why he did it; in fact, it was a dangerous—and stupid—thing to do. Someone might see him, might report him to the police. How would he explain himself?

There was no way. He no longer made house calls, so he couldn't use that as an excuse. He must be careful. Saturday was fast approaching, and he must do nothing that would jeopardize that.

But he was compelled. He thought of her face . . . so pretty . . . of that look . . . of those dark depths in her eyes . . . thought of himself falling into that gaze, falling and falling and—

As he looked out of his office window, he drummed his fingertips on the surface of the desk. He'd had his receptionist cancel most of his appointments earlier today so that now his afternoon was free.

Except that he wasn't free. He was entangled in thoughts of the girl, of that day she had visited him. His dreams were filled with the look in her big eyes, and now he was beginning to wake up in the middle of the night, unable to go back to sleep, able to see in his mind only her face, her eyes. Somehow she had completely enthralled him.

The drumming increased.

He rose to his feet and paced around for a while, but that did nothing to ease the tension inside him, so he sat back down. He looked out the window again, but really didn't see anything there.

He could see nothing, think of nothing but Jessie Morrison.

The girl and how she had looked at him.

There was something different about her, something that had imprisoned him.

Something must be done.

Something must be done to erase that expression from his mind.

Toward the end of her PE class Jessie began to feel slightly breathless, even though she wasn't exerting herself all that vigorously, and she was afraid she was going to be sick. Then she realized what was happening. She tried to even her breathing, tried hard, but it wasn't working very well.

She knew she was getting one of her spells, and she could have cried at the thought. She and the others were outside, and she looked around wildly, half expecting to see a silver Mercedes in the parking lot.

She saw nothing.

Nothing except grayness.

Not now. Not now. Not now, she screamed silently.

But she had no choice.

Well, she might suspect Marek was lying, but about what Wendy didn't really know; she had no proof, of course; just a hunch. She suspected he'd told the truth about his experiences in the camp. Surely no one could lie about that; besides, he had the tattoo to prove it.

So, what did that leave to be a lie? His experiences after the war? Working in the glassworks? His job as a journalist?

"When I still worked for the paper," Wendy said, now on her second cup of coffee, "I interviewed an old woman—a Mrs. Gottlieb who died just last year; she was truly remarkable, one of the kindest people I've ever met—who had been in the camps. She said those who gave up right away died or walked around dying with each breath."

Marek nodded. He had finished his pie and pushed the plate away and ordered more coffee for them. "What we called *mussel-men*. The walking dead."

"Mrs. Gottlieb told me she had made it through that hell only by writing detailed plays—all in her mind. At night she would lie in her bunk and write these elaborate comedies and melodramas mentally and move her characters around the stage and put in stage directions, and just ignore what went on around her."

"I've heard of that. Some of us had other forms of escape. I drew. At first, when we were in Theresienstadt, we had more belongings,

[ 105 ]

although it was never as comfortable as home, of course. But at that time I did have paper and pencils and I drew what went on around me, a sort of daily record. When I arrived at Auschwitz, I tried to get pieces of paper, but that was nearly impossible. I worked with the underground and the black market and managed to get some supplies. I drew what I saw on tatters of paper that I hid. If anyone had found them, I would doubtless have been sent to the ovens. To keep sane, my uncle completely revamped his business—all in his head, of course. It's probably one of the reasons he got back to work so soon after the war; he had his plans already diagramed out in his mind. He had only to put them down on paper afterward."

"Did you keep your sketches?"

"A few."

"But haven't put them in a book?"

"No. Others have done it, I know. Perhaps I will . . . someday. I don't think the time is right yet."

He smiled, but she saw that his eyes were dark and solemn, and there was something else deep down there, something that made her more than a little nervous, and yet which she couldn't deny also attracted her. He was charming and compelling and almost frightening, although she didn't know why.

She didn't know what it was about Marek; wasn't sure she wanted to know—but she knew she'd find out before too long.

Jessie kicked at a pebble and watched as it skittered across the sidewalk and into the gutter. She was being sent home because of her spells, dismissed from art class and geography and study hall. The note in her pocket explained that she had fainted while outside with her physical education class. The principal and her teacher thought it best if she rested for a day or two; obviously she wasn't over her illness yet.

Obviously.

Only she hadn't fainted. Not really. It had just looked that way to her teacher and the other kids when she collapsed to the ground. She could hear perfectly well what they were saying as they clustered around her, asking what had happened. And she could perfectly well hear what the others were saying, too, those nebulous voices that moaned and wept inside her head, and which were just as real as the voices of her classmates.

Now she was on her way home. She would have to show the note to her mother, and her mother would turn first red and then white, and start crying and asking where had she failed, what had she ever done to deserve this, whatever would people think, and all the while Jessie would stand there, wondering if her mother really cared about what happened to her.

Of course she does, one part of her said crossly.

I don't know.

She's your mom; of course she loves you.

Yeah, maybe, Jessie told herself. Sometimes, though, she wondered . . .

Jessie ambled along the street, then abruptly cut across an empty lot and into the woods behind it. She was in no hurry to get home right away and so she was taking a roundabout way of getting there; it was more interesting anyway than marching down the sidewalks. Plus she didn't want to see the silver Mercedes, and the car couldn't come back here.

She congratulated herself on being so clever, then giggled aloud.

Two days ago she had found an old penny along this trail and then an interesting blue glass bottle which she had washed and put on her bookcase. The penny dated from the thirties and she bet it was just about priceless; she had overheard some adults talking once about how valuable blue glass was, and she wondered if she should take it to one of the antique stores and see what they said; maybe it was a century or more older.

She liked it back here because she never knew what she would find. These woods, although not as big, reminded her of the ones not far from home in Kentucky. The woods that she and her dad had gone walking in so many times on weekends and during the summers; he would always take a sketch pad and some pencils, and sometimes they would sit for the longest time while he sketched a flower or a bird. She didn't mind sitting there, waiting, because she loved watching him, and one day he had brought along a pad of paper for her and had begun guiding her hand across the page. She had lots of her dad's sketch pads from those walks, and sometimes late at night she took them out and carefully turned the pages. She had never shown them to her mother or to Patrick, and she didn't think she ever would. Maybe one of these days she would show them to Wendy.

She sighed, thinking of her home in Lexington. She was so homesick. Sometimes the homesickness was just a big ache in her; sometimes she felt so bad she wanted to cry. Crying wouldn't help, though; it wouldn't take her back to Lexington.

She stopped and listened to a bird chirping somewhere else in the woods. She wished she could identify it. She recognized the sound of mourning doves, of course, and cardinals, and blue jays— who couldn't identify their squawking—but she didn't know much about the others. Maybe as she sketched in the woods she would learn more about the birds and other creatures that lived there.

These woods were more dangerous, her mother insisted, than those at home. The entire area around Hunters Heights was riddled with old iron mines—her mother had read this newspaper article the first day they were in Hunters Heights about the tunnels and pits out in the woods, and thereafter she had become convinced that Jessie would fall through a concealed entrance, or that their house would begin to sink into an abandoned tunnel, even though Patrick did everything he could to reassure her. He said it didn't happen very often, just once in a while. Her mother had just stared at him.

Her mother.

If she just hurried home, Jessie knew her mother would be angry at first that she was home early, then concerned, then demand to know what was wrong, and then Jessie would have to hand the note over.

She shuddered.

No, far better to take her time and just think things out first. If she got there at the regular time, maybe she wouldn't have to give her mom the note. Maybe she would forget about it by the time she got there. Yeah, she bet that would happen. She shifted her school books and grinned to herself.

A long shadow fell across the leaf-strewn path in front of her. Abruptly Jessie stopped and looked up.

The doctor stood there.

He was tall, much taller than her she remembered from the other day, and he was frowning slightly. He did not look like a frail old man to her, even though she suspected he had to be at least a hundred or so. He was dressed in regular clothes, too, so you couldn't tell he was a doctor at first glance.

He looked at her. She looked at him.

She didn't know what to say, didn't know if she could even manage to speak. She didn't like being here alone with him, in what she considered her woods, and she wished she hadn't come this way after all. She should have stuck to the sidewalks, just like her mother had always told her.

She glanced around uneasily. There was no one within sight; in fact she knew there were houses not far away, just beyond the trees, but right now she couldn't see them. She couldn't hear any sounds from the houses, either; not even any sounds of traffic, which you could always hear. All she could hear now was the trilling of some bird, and the harsh breathing of this man.

It was far too empty, far too lonely, this patch of woods.

This was worse than falling into some stupid abandoned mine, she decided, and wondered why her mother hadn't warned her about this danger. But she had. Didn't her mom always tell her not to talk to strangers? Only the awful thing was he *wasn't* a stranger.

She held her breath, waiting for him to speak first.

He stared at her, not blinking, and that made her even more uneasy. She wished he would stop looking at her.

He seemed to realize what he was doing, blinked—once, deliberate—and smiled slowly.

"I am very sorry that you were upset the other day when you came to see me in my office, Jessica. That was not my intention, you must know. I just wanted to help you."

His voice was deep and distinguished, like the voice of a politician or an actor or some guy on the radio, and for some reason the sound sent a violent shudder through her. Her body began trembling. She tried to control it, but it was impossible. She didn't want him to think she was afraid of him, even though she was. More afraid than ever before.

He saw her reaction, scowled almost as if he hadn't considered this response, and reached out with a well-kept hand as if to steady her. She took a step back, nearly stumbled, and just managed to recover her balance. Her arms felt prickly cold now.

"You don't have to be afraid."

She looked at him and his kindly face and her mouth went dry. She could see the grayness again as it threatened to completely surround her, could hear the moans and the crying, could smell that nauseating stench, and without warning she began gagging.

"Here, let me help you," he said and reached out to grasp her arm; he had no sooner touched her than abruptly the grayness snapped away, and Jessie felt a scream welling up inside, and she knew that the doctor was planning to kill her.

# NINETEEN

"*Komm hier!*"

Jessie didn't know what language he spoke. All she knew was that it was like the harsh voices she heard while she was having her spells. She didn't even think the doctor realized he wasn't speaking English.

"*Raus,*" she whispered, repeating the word she heard so often during her spells.

He blinked at her; this time he spoke in English. "What?"

"*Raus.*"

The doctor frowned, as if wondering why she was saying that word. She didn't know why she repeated it. She wondered what it meant; she had absolutely no idea, only that she heard it now and then, and that it was associated with the badness in the spell. The spell which threatened to overcome her now.

Her trembling increased as her books and notebook toppled from her numb hands, and she licked her lips and fought to keep from having a complete spell. She couldn't lose control now . . . not when he was here . . . when he could do anything while she was so helpless. The grayness . . . the sounds . . . NO!

Suddenly the doctor lunged forward and grabbed Jessie by her forearms and shook her. His grip was so tight that it hurt her arms; she tried to pull away. He clutched her even more tightly.

"Who are you?" he demanded.

Speechless, Jessie could only look up at him.

"I saw the way you stared at me Monday when you came in for the examination. Don't you think I have seen that look before?" He laughed harshly. "Well, I have. Many times, *liebchen*. Many times over the years. And I have silenced those looks many times as well. As I will with you." He drew her closer, almost as if he intended to hold her against his chest. Her cheek was so close that she would be able to hear the pounding of his heart. "You must understand I need to know more, child. Who are you that you know my secret? It is not possible! Are you a Gypsy? A Jew?"

The doctor's mouth twisted when he spoke the last word, and Jessie shivered. She had never heard such loathing.

He was pulling her toward him, closer and closer—his arms would tighten around her, and she knew she would never get loose. He would squeeze the very life from her, like a snake. She knew that.

She had to do something.

She thought of her father.

Suddenly Jessie kicked out, connecting with the man's groin. He groaned and bent over, releasing her.

Without a moment's hesitation, Jessie turned and ran. She didn't look back to see if he was chasing her. She didn't want to know. She raced through the woods, dodging this way and that, so afraid that he was only a few steps behind her, fearful that he would reach out and grab her shoulder, and he would catch her and that this time he would be *angry*.

*Raus, raus, raus,* the words whispered in her mind, and she ran as fast as she could.

Within minutes she reached Clark Street, where she risked a peek over her shoulder. No one followed. She didn't see the silver Mercedes.

Good.

Maybe she had hurt him so badly he couldn't follow. If only.

Jessie started toward her house, at a much slower pace now; she couldn't go in, with her mother there. Her mother would see how red in the face she was, and would want to know everything. And everything right now was far too complicated to explain to her mother, who would simply make it so much worse.

Jessie went around to the back and knocked on Wendy's back door.

She heard Dudley barking inside and saw one of the cats on the window. She waved to the cat, who meowed at her. No one answered.

Wendy wasn't home.

She glanced nervously at the driveway. She couldn't stay out here in the open. He might drive by any minute, and see her.

She turned around, saw the gazebo, and headed for it. The structure was mostly surrounded by thick bushes, and she could sit in it and not be seen by anyone on the street. Wendy could see her if she looked out her back window, though, like the first time she had been there.

She would be safe—for the moment. She would have to keep an eye out for the doctor, though. What if he set out on foot to search the neighborhood for her? No, she told herself. He would think she'd gone straight home, that she was in her house now; it would be the logical place for a kid to go, she reasoned. That meant she was safe here.

For now.

Jessie felt the trembling start again, and she swallowed heavily. She wanted to cry, but she couldn't. She had to be a big girl now; had to be patient and watch and make sure that the doctor didn't capture her again. That he didn't hurt her.

She wrapped her arms around herself to keep from shaking and when she looked down at her upper arms she could see the ugly bruises already forming where he had held onto her. She choked back a sob.

It was then that she realized she had dropped her schoolbooks and her notebook in the woods. She would have to return sometime to get them. She couldn't abandon them; she needed them for school.

Maybe Wendy would go with her.

She had to go to the bathroom really badly; she wished that Wendy would come home soon.

She glanced out at the street visible between the two houses, and gasped when a silver Mercedes parked in front of her house. She stepped back farther into the shadows of the gazebo. She knew she couldn't be seen here. Still . . .

The doctor got out of the car now and walked up the sidewalk to the front door. He was carrying her books and notebook.

She heard the faint ring of the bell from the open windows in her house.

"Just a moment," her mother called.

In her head she saw what was happening.

Her mother would have come downstairs, would open the door to this stranger, who would smile so politely and ask if Jessica was home. He had found her books, he would say. Her mother would begin to fret that she had lost them, and then go on and on about how careless her daughter was, and how she was always losing things, which was a lie, because Jessie never ever lost anything; her father had taught her to be careful with her belongings.

Would her mother invite him in? Jessie hoped not. What if the doctor wanted to wait for her to come home? What if he could see Wendy's backyard from where he was in the house? She would never get to leave the gazebo, not while he remained there.

What if he harmed her mother? Jessie thought suddenly, getting cold despite the warmth of the afternoon.

No, he wouldn't do that. No.

But he would have harmed *her*.

Somehow she knew there was a difference. She didn't understand it, though.

But the doctor wasn't in the house; he wasn't even staying. A minute or so later he headed back to his car, got in and drove off. She waited, but didn't see the car drive by again. Maybe he was really gone now.

Then: "Jessica Mae! Jessica Mae, where are you?" It was her mother calling.

Astrid came to the back door and called her name several times, and then started out toward Wendy's house and stopped and went back into the kitchen. Jessie knew that her mother had said she should go over and thank Wendy, but she knew her mom wouldn't. Her mom wouldn't be able to face the other woman.

She heard her mother call her several more times, and then she stopped. She supposed that she had gone back to her afternoon television programs and her ever-present ice-filled glass.

Jessie wanted to go to her, wanted her mother to put her arms around her and reassure her that everything would be all right now.

But she couldn't. She had to keep hiding.

Hiding.

Hiding from the doctor. Hiding for her life. Hiding.

She frowned at the word and something, almost a memory, flitted across her mind and she recoiled. She didn't want to know; she didn't want to remember anything because she just knew it would be unpleasant.

She heard a car again and stiffened, but this time it was Wendy's old Rabbit easing down the driveway between the houses. The car stopped and Wendy and a man got out. It was the man who had been at the diner Monday.

Wendy went to the back door and unlocked it, and the man followed her in.

Jessie didn't hesitate a moment longer. She rushed across the yard and into the house, the screen door banging shut behind her.

[ 113 ]

# TWENTY

Wendy was just putting down her purse when Jessie rushed into the kitchen. She had only a moment to register her surprise as the girl ran straight toward her and flung her arms around the older woman. Wendy put her arms around the girl and held her close, then looked across at Marek, who was equally astonished.

Jessie seemed to be crying without making a sound. When the girl's silent sobs had subsided somewhat, Wendy eased herself into a chair and pulled a tissue from her purse. She handed it to Jessie, who was sitting on her lap now. The girl dabbed at her eyes, then sniffed.

A screen door banged shut next door. "Jessica Mae! Jessica Mae!" The words were slurred.

It was Astrid Fields, and Wendy saw Jessie start visibly when she heard the sound.

"Don't tell her I'm here if she comes over, will you?" the girl pleaded.

Puzzled, Wendy nodded. "Of course not, Jessie."

After a few minutes though, Astrid Fields's voice faded. Obviously she had gone back inside the house.

Jessie continued to sit on Wendy's lap, staring down at her feet. Wendy looked over at Marek, who was still standing. He didn't look impatient or put-upon as Phil would have—Phil who would have long ago grown disgusted at the child's tears and demanded what the hell was wrong with the kid.

Quite a contrast, she thought.

"Do you want some soda, Jessie?" she asked.

The girl nodded, but when Wendy went to stand up, the girl put her arms around her.

"I'll get it," Marek said.

"Glasses are in the cabinet to the right of the stove."

He nodded and found three glasses—he selected the old jelly glasses, Wendy noted with amusement—took the bottle from the refrigerator, and poured soda for everyone. Then he closed the back door and sat in the other chair.

Wendy sipped at her soda, while Jessie ignored hers. She hadn't spoken since that one time.

"Something has deeply frightened her," Marek said as he studied the girl's face.

"What, though?" Wendy stroked Jessie's hair. "C'mon, honey, have something to drink."

Jessie muttered something so low that Wendy couldn't catch it.

"What?"

This time her voice was louder. "*Obavách.*"

Marek sat forward and peered intently at her.

"*Obavách,*" the girl whispered.

"What's she saying?" Wendy asked. "I don't know what that word is."

"I would be very surprised if you did, Wendy. Jessie is speaking Czech."

"What?" As far as she knew, the only language Jessie could speak was English.

The little girl muttered the word again and shifted on Wendy's lap.

"*Obavách* means afraid—she's fearful," he explained.

Marek began speaking to Jessie in what Wendy assumed was Czech. For the longest time the girl said nothing; finally, she answered what seemed to be his question. He talked to her some more, then she shook her head. He asked her something again, and then the girl began speaking. Sometimes she could barely choke out a word; sometimes the word turned into a sob.

Marek replied in a low soothing voice. She cocked an ear toward him and listened, and Wendy felt some of the tenseness in the child's body go away. Marek put his hand on the table, palm up, and after a few minutes Jessie placed hers on top. He did not try to hold her hand, though, which was good; Wendy suspected the girl would have shrieked had he tried. She didn't know why she thought that; she just thought that any sudden movement would terrify Jessie.

Wendy looked at him, waiting for him to explain.

"I can't make out entirely what she's saying; it doesn't make a lot of sense. Apparently earlier today something . . . someone . . .

[ 115 ]

scared her and badly, too. She ran home, but knew she couldn't hide there, it wasn't safe, and so she hid . . . her family said it was best. She hid from him . . . from them. She had to, she said; she had no other choice; but she knows they'll—he'll—find her eventually." He frowned.

"What's the matter?"

"I don't know. There's something about the words." He spoke to Jessie again softly, in Czech, but she didn't answer. Wendy saw the girl's eyes had closed.

"I think she's fallen asleep. Maybe I should put her on the couch where she can sleep."

Marek nodded. "I'll do it."

He lifted the girl easily, and followed Wendy into the living room, where he settled the girl onto the couch. Wendy laid one of the crocheted afghans there across Jessie to keep her warm; it wasn't a cold day, but Jessie had suffered some sort of a shock, and she would need to stay warm. Almost immediately the tiny black cat jumped up and curled up at the girl's feet. Dudley flopped down on the floor alongside the couch.

Wendy glanced out the window at the street as a car drove by. It was Mr. Johnstone from up the street, home early from work. She went across the room and pulled the drapes shut; for some reason, she didn't want them open. She felt vulnerable, with the girl lying there on the couch.

Who could see? What did it matter? she asked herself.

She watched the child for a few minutes longer and when Jessie didn't stir she returned to the kitchen. Marek was leaning against the stove, staring out the back window.

"What do you think?" she asked.

He glanced at her. "I don't know. I know that it is impossible for a child her age to speak such good Czech without having lived there. Yet I doubt she has."

"No; they're from Kentucky."

"Those words . . . something about hiding. It bothers me, and I don't know why."

Wendy was glad now that on the spur of the moment at the Iron Forge she'd invited Marek back to the house. She had said they could take her car, and later return for his. She had enjoyed their lunch and discussion, and didn't want it to end. In the car they'd talked about why she was no longer a reporter, and he had asked many intelligent questions about her writing. Perhaps she wanted

[116]

to show him her office and what she had done there. Perhaps there was another motivation—although she wasn't sure of that.

She didn't think she was so starved for attention and company that she invited men she scarcely knew back to her house so that she could jump into the sack with them. At least she believed that wasn't her motivation. Phil would have thought so, she knew, and had accused her on more than one occasion of such a thing.

But then he accused her of many things—things that he himself was in fact doing.

She sighed.

"Shouldn't you call her mother to let her know her daughter is here?"

"I should, but I'm not going to. Astrid is . . . um, how shall I say this? A less-than-attentive mother. When Jessie got sick Monday—and I'm pretty sure it was just first-day jitters—her mother had no idea the girl wasn't feeling well. Jessie came to me, not to her. That says something about Astrid, I think. Jessie has said a few things about her folks—her dad is dead—and she's none too happy with her stepfather. I don't know that he hits her, but frankly I wouldn't put it past him. I heard what I thought were screams one night and couldn't figure out where they came from, and the more I think about it the more I think it was from next door."

"Did you see the bruises on the girl's arms?"

She nodded. She had noticed them right away and wondered what could have marked the child. They were not the sort of bruises a kid got scrambling around and playing. They looked like bruises from fingers, as if someone had gripped her hard. Who had hurt the girl so?

"Maybe someone tried to kidnap her," Marek suggested after a moment. He came to the table and sat, and Wendy thought he looked weary for some reason.

"It could be. I've heard of such things—you read about it in the paper ever so often, although mostly in big cities like New York. I don't understand them, but I guess no reasonable person does."

"Those bruises will heal eventually," he said.

She thought suddenly of what he had talked about at lunch; she pictured him as a youth confined in a Nazi death camp, and hundreds of thousands, millions perhaps, of innocent children who had gone to their deaths there in Auschwitz and the other concentration camps. How could any reasonable person have understood that?

[ 117 ]

"I should go," he announced suddenly.

"I'll drive you back."

"No, you stay with Jessie. I think she needs you to be here when she wakes up. You two are going to have to come up with quite a story for her mother. You're a fiction writer, so this should not be such a difficult thing." He smiled.

"Fiction writer, not liar." But she smiled too.

"I'll walk," he said. "The exercise will do be me good."

"Thank you for coming back to the house, Stefan. I'm sorry about what happened."

"Don't be sorry. I'll come by again. Tomorrow perhaps? I think I would like to talk to Jessie when she is feeling better."

"Good."

Marek nodded to her and went out the back door, closing it softly so as not to wake Jessie, even though Wendy wasn't sure anything could do that right now.

As she peered into the living room at the sleeping child, Wendy began to suspect there was a lot more to this than Jessie simply being scared. What, though, she didn't know.

When Jessie woke it was almost dark, and she didn't know where she was or what had happened. As she shifted her arm dangled over the edge of the couch. Her fingers touched something warm and furry, and then suddenly a dog's tongue licked her hand.

She giggled. It was Dudley.

Suddenly she remembered what had happened. She had seen the doctor in the woods and he had grabbed her but she had managed to get away and she had run to Wendy's and then she had come in here, and Wendy and that foreign guy were in the kitchen and then— and then she didn't remember.

She probably had one of her spells, she thought with embarrassment. She would have to try to explain to Wendy. Otherwise her friend would think she was a real spaz or something.

She could hear the woman moving around in the kitchen, trying to be quiet. Wendy had a radio on low and it was playing "Rhinestone Cowboy," the new song from Glen Campbell. She liked the song, even though her mother said rock 'n' roll was the devil's instrument. It was a good thing that her mother wasn't seriously religious.

Jessie felt a furry bundle on her feet shift and stretch, heard a yawn, and then the cat settled back down on her feet. Dudley licked her fingers again, and Jessie yawned.

*Dobry.* Good.

She didn't realize she had spoken aloud.

She should go in and talk to Wendy. Then she should go home. Right now she was still tired. Maybe she would doze again, and then she would get up. She was getting kind of hungry, too. Sleep. Just a bit . . . just for a few . . . minutes . . .

Dudley licked the sleeping girl's face, but she didn't wake up, and after a while he settled back down alongside the couch and was soon snoring.

# TWENTY-ONE

Thorne paced around the den, wondering where the child could have gone. He'd had a grip on her so tight she couldn't break away, and then the little bitch had kicked him in the balls.

He had tried to follow, but he had been hobbled by the pain in his groin and fell farther and farther behind. Finally, he had given up and returned to pick up the stuff she had dropped.

He stopped moving and stared down at the carpet.

Not knowing what else to do, he had driven to her house and rung the doorbell, and when her mother—an inferior-looking creature, if he ever saw one, and he had seen many in his life—had finally shuffled to the door, he had explained that he had found Jessica's books and notebook. The mother had said her daughter wasn't home yet, and he didn't think she was lying. Why should she, after all? He doubted she had the intelligence to do such a thing.

Then he said he was the doctor who had seen her the other day, and he expressed his hope that Jessica was feeling much better.

The mother had murmured that she was.

Even through the screen door, which the woman had kept firmly latched, he could smell the alcohol on the woman's breath. She wouldn't know where her daughter was, he thought contemptuously, because she was too interested in her own problems and was attempting to drown her unhappiness with the bottle. A drunken slattern, he decided. Thirty-five years ago this woman would have been sent east, and she would have deserved it. She wouldn't have lasted long; she didn't have what it took to survive; few did, that's why they had died by the millions. He could tell just by looking at Astrid. He curled his lip in disgust.

The woman had tried to ask him in, but he had said he had

[ 120 ]

business elsewhere. When he got into his car and looked back, he had seen her still at the door. He figured she would have gone straight back to her soap operas and ice-filled glass.

Jessica, he thought with surprise, did not seem much like her mother. The girl had spunk, unlike the mother. But Jessica now . . . he was determined to find her. And very soon. They had some unfinished business, these two.

Jessie took a big bite of the grilled cheese sandwich Wendy had prepared.

It was dark now, and she would have to go home real soon and face her mother and Patrick. But she was ready; she had a story prepared. She had thought about it right after Wendy had awakened her.

"This is good."

"I'm glad you like it."

Wendy had been real good about not asking a lot of questions; her mother would have kept after her, asking question after question.

"You won't tell my mom, will you?" she asked suddenly, her hand halfway to the tumbler filled with milk.

"Not unless you want me to."

Jessie shook her head. "Not yet. She wouldn't understand. And she gets real upset about things real easily. My dad said she was high-strung."

Wendy just smiled.

Jessie knew that the woman expected her to tell her what happened. She wanted to . . . but . . . she wasn't sure she could explain it. What if she said that the doctor who had looked at her Monday had tried to do something to her? Wendy wouldn't believe her. After all, Wendy had seen her sort of freak out in his office. She would think Jessie was naming him because of that; she thought her friend who had been to the shrink called it association. Or something like that.

Besides, no one ever believed kids, and as much as she liked Wendy, she had to remind herself that she was an adult, and thus it was pretty likely she wouldn't believe her.

Jessie finished her sandwich and her milk, patted Dudley on his head, then stood up.

"I'd better go."

"All right. Come back tomorrow after school, if you want, Jessie. I think Stefan is coming by, and he'd like to talk with you."

She shrugged. "Sure. If I'm not grounded for life." Then she grinned to let Wendy know that she didn't mean it. She waved and left, and circled around Wendy's house so that she could come up her own sidewalk—as if she were coming from someplace else.

She took a deep breath and went inside.

Patrick was waiting in the living room. Her mom was in a chair, just sitting and looking at nothing. He looked worried and angry all at once; her mother looked like she had been crying. Jessie felt bad; but there was no way she could have come home any sooner.

Patrick stood, the better, she supposed, to look down at her and make her feel small. He was in his business suit yet, which meant he had probably just gotten home and hadn't bothered to change.

"It's after eight o'clock at night. Where have you been, young lady?"

Jessie glanced at her mom, then at Patrick, and tried to look surprised. "I was studying at a friend's, and it got late and they invited me for supper. Then I came home. Honest."

"Why didn't you call?" he demanded.

"I didn't think I had to." She went on quickly before he could say anything. "I told Mom about this yesterday." She hated to lie, but she had no choice; it was her only way out of this.

Patrick looked over at her mom to see what she would say. Astrid blinked, and Jessie knew that her mom could recall no such thing but was afraid to admit it.

"I remember that now. I should have remembered, honey. I guess I thought that was tomorrow."

Jessie nodded, but felt terrible. Her mom was trying to be nice, and here she was lying to her. But she *had* to. Had, had, had to.

"Some guy came by earlier and brought your books here. How'd you come to lose them?"

Jessie shrugged offhandedly. Her heart beat wildly when Patrick mentioned the doctor. But he didn't say that, did he? And she must remember not to accidentally call him that, or they would both know something was up. "Some kid at school took them."

"Why?"

"Why do boys do any of the dumb things they do, Patrick? He was showing off or something. Just being real stupid, you know."

She waited. Would he believe? And what if he didn't? Would he hit her? He hadn't—yet. Inside she trembled, and her hands felt sweaty.

Patrick grunted, then walked into the kitchen. He didn't come back, so Jessie assumed that everything was okay; he must believe her then. She went to her mother and put her arms around her and hugged her tightly.

"I'm sorry I worried you, Mom. I didn't mean to."

Astrid patted her arm. "I know you didn't, honey. I know. It's just that I get so forgetful now and then, you know."

Tears stung Jessie's eyes, and she bit her lip so she wouldn't cry. Her mother stroked her hair and for a few minutes they stayed that way. It was nice, Jessie thought, being this close to her again, without her fretting. She hugged her closer.

Then: "You coming or what, Astrid? Dinner's getting cold."

Jessie drew away and awkwardly patted her mother's shoulder. Suddenly she felt much older than her mother. She realized too that her mother wasn't as tall as she used to be, and that made her sad. "You'd better go in, Mom. Okay?"

Astrid nodded and stood, somewhat unsteadily, and Jessie walked with her into the kitchen. Patrick was already eating and he didn't bother looking up when they entered. Her mother eased herself into a chair and Jessie dished out some food and put it in front of her mother.

"You're mother isn't an invalid, Jess," Patrick said, around a mouthful of mashed potatoes. "She can damned well help herself."

"I was just being polite," she said. "My dad always said we should help others."

"Your dad." He made a noise and smirked down at the peas he was mixing with his mashed potatoes.

"What about my dad?" she said slowly. Her hands clenched at her sides.

Patrick opened his mouth, but her mother spoke first.

"Patrick, not tonight."

Her stepfather looked at her, then down at his plate again, and shrugged.

Jessie fixed a small plate of food for herself; she wasn't all that hungry, but thought she better eat whatever she could, even though she'd already had a sandwich and had supposedly had dinner at a friend's.

They ate in silence for a while, which pleased Jessie. She didn't want to have to try to talk to either tonight. She just wasn't in the mood.

"What happened to your arms?" he asked when he had helped himself to another pork chop. He nodded at the bruises, so dark against her skin.

She looked down at them, shrugged casually. "I guess I got them at school somehow. Maybe in PE, out on the playing field."

"Yeah?"

"Yeah." She stared him in the eye, daring him to contradict her. He didn't.

Her mother continued to eat, her head bowed.

No one spoke for the rest of the meal, for which she was grateful, and when she asked to be excused and was granted permission, Jessie took her plate to the sink and rinsed it off. Then she picked up her books lying in the living room and headed up the stairs.

"Jess."

She looked down to see Patrick standing at the bottom of the stairs. He was wiping his mouth on a paper napkin, and when he was done, he balled it up.

"Yeah?"

"You're taking a shower tonight."

She thought of all that she had gone through that day, thought of the note that she hadn't given her mother yet, of the fear she had felt when she faced the doctor, and she stared down at him.

"No."

He blinked, and without another word she turned, went into her room, and locked the door.

# TWENTY-TWO

Marek had given up watching early. The doctor's pattern had been the same the last few nights. Home from work around eight or nine, dinner downstairs, an hour or so of television, up to bed to read for another hour, and then the light off, always by midnight.

Unfailingly.

So Marek had called it quits. He was tired, more tired than he would like to admit. He had done this sort of thing for many years now, but he wasn't as young as he had been, and all the trailing and intrigue . . . he thought it might be taking a bit of a toll.

Or possibly not, he thought with a wry smile.

He kicked off his shoes and padded around in his stocking feet for a while, moving things, picking up clothing he'd left draped over chairs in the morning when he left in a hurry. He checked to make sure that nothing important had been disturbed and was reassured to find it hadn't. He supposed the maid that Mrs. Addison had for the inn simply came in and made the bed and vacuumed the rug and changed the towels. If that.

He had specified a bathroom with his room. Not all came with one, but he had wanted it. Normally he wouldn't have minded sharing—he had done it often enough in the past—but this time he required the privacy. He went in now and turned on the tap and let the water run until it was really cold, then he held the glass under it and drank first one glassful, then another. He filled the glass a third time and bought it back into the bedroom and set it down on the bedside table.

He should have stopped at a liquor store for something stronger, except that he never drank alcohol while working. It didn't make good business sense. At least he could have picked up some sodas. Still, the water would do. Certainly he had drunk far worse.

He took out his suitcase again, and lifted out an attaché case. He unlocked it, and removed the manila folders and large envelopes, and placed them on the bed as he sat cross-legged on the quilt.

"A genuine Amish handmade quilt from Lancaster Pee-Ay," he remembered Mrs. Addison declaring, the day she had shown him the room, as if that would settle his decision on taking the room. He thought the coverlet quite nice, but frankly it had nothing to do with his selection of the room. He wanted this room because of the view of town he had from the window.

He opened the first folder and studied the photocopies of pass-ports and medical records and insurance card and social security card and credit references and college degrees and transcripts. All the documentation for a new life. He reread the letters he had read dozens of times before, sifted through the testimony of the old local woman his uncle had contacted him about. The reason for his being in Hunters Heights now.

He drank the water slowly as he looked through the other folders, filled with sheet after sheet of the typed testimony of dozens of witnesses, snippets of conversations, remembrances of another time, another life. He arranged the photographs—those clipped from newspapers and magazines as well as duplicated prints—in two rows. From young man to old man; there was no doubt it was the same person.

Angrily Marek thrust the glossies back into the folders, and pulled out one of the large envelopes. He opened the clasp and drew out the photos carefully, as if fearing that to touch them would somehow destroy them.

They were photographs of people—men and women being herded into long lines before the *Selektion*, of bodies stacked one upon each other like logs in a cord of wood, of men grim-faced pointing at the brick ovens for the camera's unflinching eye. Men and women and children, bereft of their clothing and their dignity, lined up in front of ditches, soon to be their burial place. Men hanging from electrified barbed wire like desiccated scarecrows. Dozens of people standing and sitting and milling around, with lost eyes and lost souls. Mounds of hats and boots and coats and prosthetic limbs; hills of dolls and teddy bears and purses and wallets and brassieres. Piles of eyeglasses, and gold and silver pulled from teeth, of shaven hair of dead women used to stuff the mat-tresses upon which the German citizens slept. Women with skin stretched so tautly across their faces that they were scarcely more than rictal skulls, sexless now. Skeletal children, wizened beyond their years, who had long ago been stripped of their youth.

It was hard to tell the living from the dead.

The second envelope contained crumbling papers. There were bits and scraps of different textures and sizes, all drawings he had made while in Auschwitz. The barracks where he lived; the tiers of bunks inside; the factory he had worked in; the steps down to the dressing rooms and beyond that the shower room; the brick ovens. Some were drawn roughly upon the backside of light-colored material. He picked up one small sketch, done with the stub of a pencil he had somehow obtained through the black market, and the scrap crumbled. He tucked the sketches away and knew that he would never be able to look at them again.

A third envelope contained more photographs. The first was old; he had been only seven, and Tomáš had just turned two, and his mother stood with Tomáš in her arms, and her belly bulged with her pregnancy. In a few months Eduard would be born. His mother smiled shyly at the camera; his father grinned, and why not? He led a good life, had a beautiful and intelligent wife, a third child upon the way, what could go wrong?

Another picture showed the Mareks together: Stefan's father and his two uncles; his mother and his aunt not yet pregnant with the child that would never be born; Stefan and his brothers; his three little girl cousins, Ružena the eldest, Helenka the middle daughter, and Anna the baby; his grandfather and grandmother; and Rabbi Zucker, whose normally gentle face looked so solemn for Uncle Karel's bar mitzvah.

It was the last time the immediate family would be together for such a celebration. Shortly after this Karel would be sent abroad to study, the Nazis would invade Czechoslovakia, and his family's descent into hell would begin.

Stefan had never had a bar mitzvah. His thirteenth birthday in Auschwitz had been a day much like the thousand others he endured in the concentration camp; a day where morning and night he devoured a bowl of greasy gruel with something dark floating in it—one didn't question what the substance might be; it was food, after all—the chronic thirst, the back-breaking labor, not enough sleep; and always it was too cold or too hot, too dry or too wet. No flowers bloomed within sight of the camp; there was nothing but the bleak, endless brown and gray of barrack after barrack. Only at night did color appear, in the yellow and orange flames of the ravenous ovens. He wondered if the ashy residue that settled upon the forests surrounding the camp killed the trees.

Suddenly he swept all the photos from the bed and put his hands up to his face. But he could not cry.

As she lay in bed Wendy reviewed the day. It had been a packed one. She was accustomed to days a bit more quiet: usually she had breakfast, worked, lunched, got back to work and somewhere along the way broke for dinner, and then either worked at night or read. Today had definitely been different.

First, there had been the chance encounter at the supermarket, which she actually doubted was as happenstance as Marek would have her believe. Why he would seek her out, though, she couldn't imagine. And then had come the lunch with him, which she had enjoyed—almost too much, one part of her chided—and then this whole weird incident with Jessie.

She had wanted nothing more than to ask the girl who had scared her so much; several times she'd been on the verge while Jessie ate her sandwich. Wendy also knew that kids tended to clam up when adults pressed them for details. Adults pried; or at least that's what kids believed. So she had kept her mouth shut. It had been hard, though.

She believed, however, that Jessie would tell her when she was good and ready; and in the meantime she'd keep an eye out for her as much as possible.

And if something happens? one part of her asked. What then? You might be able to prevent it if you had all the facts.

If.

But nothing will happen. Nothing. Maybe if Wendy repeated it enough to herself it would become real.

For some reason the thought left her uneasy.

She sighed as she watched light reflected from a car's headlights inch across the ceiling of her bedroom, and she thought not for the first time how big and how lonely was her bed.

It might not have been this afternoon, she told herself, and found she was blushing.

So, you think you could have seduced him? she asked herself. She almost laughed aloud. Right. Phil said she couldn't charm anyone with either her words or her looks. But then he'd always had a way of pricking her ego. Never mind that he didn't keep his in check.

But, she asked herself, what if . . . what if Marek had stayed? She had planned on showing him her office and her novels and maybe they would have gotten to talking again, and she might have fixed them some dinner, and then what if he had stood up and suddenly bent and kissed her?

What if, indeed?

What if she had moved into his arms very naturally, and what if the next thing she knew they were in her bed, making love?

Dudley whined in his sleep.

With a dog howling outside the door, she thought with a sudden grin.

And yet . . . what if?

There's still tomorrow, she told herself, and in that moment she realized just how much she needed someone's arms around her. She hadn't slept with anyone since Phil had moved out. That had been a while. It was a long time without love.

Too long.

Wendy closed her eyes and pretended to sleep, no matter that she no longer felt sleepy.

# TWENTY-THREE

He dreamed of the camp as he had not done in years.

Once more he was stumbling off the train, glad to be able to stretch and stand fully erect and to be finally rid of the all-too-human smells that had surrounded him for days. Surely now that they were . . . wherever . . . they would be allowed to bathe, to change their clothing, to eat and drink, to sleep in a real bed instead of standing or sitting the way they had. Surely someone would explain what was happening.

Surely.

Still, he was so thirsty, had been for days now; his lips like paper, his tongue feeling swollen. Others had complained during the train ride of that horrible dryness, but he had never said a word. He couldn't, not when others around him suffered more.

There had been a precious little water to go around in the first place—who had thought to pack that, and the train certainly hadn't stopped so they could drink—and he had given up his share so that his grandfather might have something more to drink. The old man, too ill to do anything but huddle on a crate in a corner of the too-crowded boxcar and pray in a low voice, had clasped his hand before the train had finally come to a halt and stroked it once. And he had known then with terrible certainty that his grandfather would not live long.

Now, he and his parents and his two younger brothers were outside, and none of them could figure out where they were, what they were doing here. Everything had been so puzzling since they had been forced from their comfortable home months ago in Prague, forced to leave in the middle of the night as if they were criminals, forced to leave only with the clothes on their back and what few belongings they could scramble together in half an hour.

Just follow the rules, his father had urged as they tumbled from the cattle cars. This is probably all some sort of bureaucratic snarl.

Follow the rules. Fine if you knew what the rules were.

Follow the rules, his father had counseled, as they were sent from Prague to Theresienstadt, and now his father said the same thing.

What rules? Whose rules?

And where in God's name were they?

They had listened to his father, had followed the rules and arrived, in the middle of the night, in some alien place with lights so bright he had to squint to see, and there were the harsh sounds of men shouting in Polish and German, dogs barking, sobbing, ghastly flames that rose into the black sky, oily ashes that settled upon his cheeks and lips and made him rub his hand violently against his mouth, and above all a stench that made him want to throw up.

"*Raus, raus, raus!*" men in striped pajamas with shaved heads who looked like common criminals yelled in German. He knew German; it would have been impossible not to know because he grew up in Prague, a city filled with Germans. *Move it, hurry, quick now.*

Hurry for what? he wondered.

He stared around him in confusion, as did the others, and he watched as the men in striped pajamas, these kapos, shoved the new arrivals here and there, so that they formed two lines, one of men and boys, the other of women and girls.

The new arrivals, still dazed, stumbled forward, and watched as the kapos seized the meager baggage they had brought with them, watched numbly as the bodies of those who had died on the rail journey were tossed out of the boxcars and piled on a wagon.

Then the kapos pushed them forward, and the long lines plodded before armed men in SS uniforms and the doctor, who flicked a finger left or right.

The *Selektion.*

To the right went those who were to live—for a while—those who would be the slaves of the labor camp of Auschwitz-Birkenau, the healthy middle-aged men and women, the boys who looked strong. Just as he had until the camp was liberated by the Russians three years later, in January of 1945.

To the left went the old, the useless, the weak, the ill, pregnant women, mothers with small children or infants in arms, those who

[ 131 ]

looked older than their years. Those who couldn't labor for the Third Reich.

He had never had a chance to say good-bye to his mother, to his brothers, to his grandfather and grandmother. His aunt, big in belly with her unborn child, carried one little girl, while her mother carried one of his girl cousins; the third, the oldest one—the one they had tried to save by hiding in another part of Prague but who had been discovered and returned to her family—walked behind. He had only one last glimpse of them as he spun around and raised one hand, and his mother had flashed a brave smile while his one brother helped his grandfather because the man couldn't walk on his own, and then a man had stepped forward and shoved his mother, and she had stumbled, and they were out of his sight.

He had wanted to run after her, but couldn't. He had wanted to cry, but couldn't; never during those years he endured in Auschwitz had he cried, and he had wondered as he looked around at the other men and boys who cried why he didn't.

Perhaps something had shriveled inside him that night when he saw his family for the last time. Perhaps.

Or perhaps he had cried continually inside all those years.

Above all this confusion and noise, he could still remember the lilting music of the camp orchestra, forced to play for the new arrivals. To show these bewildered newcomers that life was fine here. Polkas and waltzes and jazz and show tunes . . . bright lively music. All of it a lie.

From there he and his father and uncle and the other dazed men walked down a road. Past the brick building where the hideous flames shot upward. Here the nauseatingly sweet smell was strongest, and here he gagged, putting his hand over his nose, but even that didn't keep the cloying odor out.

The camp bakery, they were told, unaware of the hideous irony.

They marched to an iron gate, which swung open. Above the gate a sign read *"Arbeit Macht Frei."* Work Makes You Free.

From there they filed into a vast building, where they were ordered to strip. As they stood, naked and embarrassed, trying in vain to cover their genitals, he and his father and uncle had looked around and he knew they all thought the same thing: what have we done to deserve this treatment?

They never knew; never.

From there they stepped into another part of the building, where barbers shaved their heads, the hair under their arms and in their groin. An acrid-smelling blue paste was dabbed on the shaved areas.

To delouse them, they were told.

We've never had lice, his father protested, but one of the kapos clubbed him in the face with his fist. His father fell back, and he grabbed his arm so that he wouldn't be hurt again.

They were handed clothing, or far more accurately, rags. Some men had formal pants, the stiff creases still evident; others had casual dungarees, while still some wore what looked like pajama bottoms. The size of clothing mattered not at all to the guards; loose clothing was given to short skinny youths; tight clothing to the larger men. Some were handed white T-shirts to wear as tops; others were given thick flannel shirts. Still others had shirts with holes at the elbows or in the back. Some men had belts for their pants; others didn't. They were given boots and shoes and sandals to wear. Most of the time the shoes didn't fit, but he figured he was lucky to have them at all.

The wrong size, the lack of decent clothing, this utter confusion of the senses—it didn't matter in this topsy-turvy world. At least not to their captors.

To him and the other men and boys it was simply one more thing to perplex them.

On their clothing in the front was sewn a triangle with the letter C. C for Czech, P for Polish, R for Russian. So very efficient, these Nazis, to devise a system by which they could tell at a glance to what group a prisoner belonged; so much more handy than papers. The color of the triangle announced the type of prisoner: common criminals wore a green triangle, prostitutes a black one, a yellow trim for Jews such as he and his family and their neighbors, as well as a stripe of red down the back.

In the next part of the building, he and his father and the other men encountered more German bureaucracy. Some men sat behind an extended table; none of them smiled; and they were writing on pads of paper. He was pushed forward, his arm grabbed and held down on the cold surface of the table, and before he could protest or struggle they had tattooed a number in blue ink on the inside of his left forearm.

He had remembered the pain and the abrupt strangeness and surprise of this inexplicable deed and had wanted to cry, but couldn't. He had watched as boys his age cried, and men twice his age sobbed.

Still, he couldn't. All he could do was cradle his arm and remember the pain.

From there he and the men and boys went into the camp proper. From that moment on the nightmare, the living hell began, and he moaned as he slept, unaware of the whimpering sounds he made.

He dreamed of the camp as he had not done in years.

He remembered watching the two lines of pitiful derelicts that dared to call themselves human as they shuffled forward, their heads hung in misery. Gypsies and Jews and the Slavs and social democrats and homosexuals and Communists and trade unionists and Roman Catholic nuns and priests and all the other undesirables ferreted out by the Reich.

All the living trash of the earth.

He was newly appointed, and if he had ever felt horror at what happened there, it had quickly died—as quickly as those interred there died. He had worked with the Great Doctor in his noble experiments; he had learned much in those days as a young doctor.

He remembered the lengthy line to the left and how the men and women and children cried as they inched toward their fate. He had looked at them with scorn; they could not even go to their deaths with dignity.

Those who suspected what waited for them in the brick shower room whimpered and sometimes one got out of line and tried to grab his arm and beg for mercy, but the SS guards always moved in and shoved the momentary protestor back into line. With the other debris.

These derelicts were escorted by the SS to a long underground viaduct which led to the undressing room. There they found signs in various languages, placed to reassure them that they were to hang their clothing on the hooks and could later claim it.

From there the naked people—men and women and children all together—were herded briskly and without ceremony into a low, narrow shower room. Then the doors were slammed shut and locked.

Too late they suspected. If you stood close enough, he recalled, you could hear the shouts and screams of those who wanted out, of their pounding fists on the door as they pressed against it in the darkness.

Dumb as animals, he and the other Germans had often joked. Dumber, some claimed.

The Germans always waited a while before releasing the gas. Scientists had discovered that for the gas to work most efficiently the temperature of the room had to be raised a few degrees, and while the humans screamed in the cramped room, the temperature rose, fouling the air.

And then the SS guard, protected in his gas mask, would open the peephole in the ceiling and drop in the cylinder of the gas Zyklon B.

When it was over the doors were opened, and a special unit of prisoners, the *Sonderkommando*, used special hook-tipped poles which were thrust deep into the flesh of the dead people to pull them out of the room. German scientists had invented these tools so that the process might go more efficiently. Often the bodies were jumbled together at the door end of the room, limbs broken, small children trampled on the bottom. Once the dead were broken apart, the men of the *Sonderkommando* shaved the hair of the dead and extracted the gold and silver from their mouths. Only then were they transported to the ovens. Often there were those still breathing among the dead. They too were shoved into the ovens; dead or alive, it didn't matter. The Nazis in their practical way had discovered the most efficient way to operate the ovens. First, babies were tossed in as kindling, followed by the most emaciated bodies of former inmates, then finally those of the larger adults to feed the flames.

Thousands fueled the fire every hour; every hour of every day; every day of every year for nearly four years. In one camp alone.

It was, he had said then and since, a model of Reich efficiency. German engineering and great capability, which had gone on to produce some of the best cars and stereos and cameras in the world. It could all be traced back to those days.

He rolled over, one hand cradled beneath his head, and smiled as he slept.

Jessie lay awake, unable to sleep. She was afraid that if she fell asleep, the awful dreams would come again, and her spells would start all over. What if somehow she got caught in those dreams, what if she couldn't get out, couldn't get back again?

She shuddered.

She didn't know that it could happen, although it might be possible.

She touched the ring on the chain around her neck, as if that might somehow reassure her, but tonight it was simply metal.

She lay for a few more minutes, sleep no closer, and finally decided to get up. She went across to the window and looked out. Wendy's house was dark. She was in bed already.

Jessie felt slightly let down; she had hoped to see a light on; she would have found it reassuring. It would have been like she and Wendy were somehow communicating, or maybe that Wendy was somehow watching out for her.

Now there was nothing but darkness.

She held her breath, listening, but even the normal sounds of night were gone. She didn't hear any tree peepers or crickets; not even the bark of a lone dog.

Nothing.

Quietly she pulled a chair to the window and sat, then tried to peer out at the street, but she couldn't see it from where she sat, not really.

Did someone stand out there even now, watching her house? Did *he* stand out there, hidden by the darkness?

She wondered if she should turn on the porch light. That might scare him away. If he was there. Or he might realize it was her, and he might come to the door and—

And she would scream if she saw him. She'd scream loud and long, and Patrick and her mother would come running downstairs right away and turn on the lights so that all the shadows fled, and Patrick would demand to know what was going on, and her mother would look so scared, and Jessie would say there had been a man outside the house, and Patrick would demand to know what the hell she'd been doing up at this time of night, and her mother would start to cry and—

No, she'd better not turn on the light.

She couldn't turn her light on in her room so she could read or draw. He might see. She could close the windows and pull the shades down and close the curtains tightly, but there would still be light that spilled out of the house, around the shade and the curtains. And he would know.

He might come and stand beneath her window.

She closed her eyes at that thought.

And continued to sit and watch all through the night. Toward dawn, still in the chair, her arms wrapped around her legs, Jessie slept finally, without dreams.

# THURSDAY

# TWENTY-FOUR

Marek came by Wendy's house in the afternoon. For a while he chatted with Jessie, sometimes in English, sometimes in Czech. She seemed so unaware of what language she was speaking she went from one to the other without pausing.

Right now she was sitting at the kitchen table with a pad of paper in front of her, holding a colored pencil in her right hand. She was concentrating on a picture she wanted to do for Wendy, she had said.

"What did she say, Stefan?" Wendy asked. She thought he seemed particularly quiet today. When he had arrived, he had been frowning slightly and looked like he hadn't gotten much rest the night before. Jessie looked like she hadn't slept much, either.

Marek had brushed off her concern with an abrupt wave of his hand and a wordless grunt, and Wendy had wondered about that; previously he had been unfailingly polite. Something was obviously bothering him; but it was also apparent he wasn't going to discuss it.

"The things she has spoken of—" He looked away, looked out the window. Then he shrugged. "I don't know how she could know them."

"Know what?"

The details of last night's dream were all too clear in his mind; perhaps he was somehow overlaying them onto what the child said. Perhaps she hadn't spoken of such things at all.

No, he wasn't imagining it. She had said what she had said. However impossible that could be.

"Jessica."

The girl looked up and smiled at him.

It was obvious that Jessie liked and trusted Marek, and Wendy thought that was a good thing. She liked him, too. Trusted? She wasn't sure about that, and she didn't understand why. There seemed more to Marek than he was saying. Was that such a bad thing? one part of her wondered. She didn't know.

"I would like to talk to you again," he said gently, sitting in a kitchen chair opposite her.

Jessie put down the pencil and nodded.

Marek glanced at the picture she had been working on and then froze momentarily. "May I?" he asked, indicating the pad. She nodded, and he pulled the paper around so that Wendy could see.

Wendy glanced down at the picture and couldn't believe what she saw.

There on the stark white page Jessie had drawn a barbed-wire fence, and behind it stood men, women, and a handful of children, all painfully thin, all dressed in rags, all with faces filled with despair. Their eyes were large and blackened, empty of life. Some sagged against the fence, obviously dead. Behind these pitiful relics rose the arch of a gate, and its crudely lettered words read "*Arbeit Macht Frei.*"

Wendy had heard of that cruelly ironic phrase, knew what that meant from her research. It was the slogan, if one could call it that, of the death camps of the Nazis during World War II. Work makes you free—because in those camps it killed you. Wendy knew it; but how could a little girl like Jessie know it? Wendy was convinced that neither Jessie's parents nor stepfather had ever mentioned the concentration camps to this child. That had happened long ago in another country, Americans were wont to believe; it can't happen here. So why bring up all that unpleasantness again?

"This is a very good sketch," Marek said. "It is very accurate. Did you know that?"

Jessie shook her head.

"May I look at your other sketches?" She nodded, and he began flipping through the pad. He paused to show some of them to Wendy.

One was a picture of a brick chimney and from the top spewed forth flames which Jessie had colored yellow and orange. She had drawn dots around the flames, and Wendy thought that must be ash, but when she stepped closer and peered over Marek's shoulder, she could see that the dots were the faces of people. Another sketch showed a train, its boxcars crammed to overflowing with people. Yet another showed a man in a striped uniform beating a woman holding an infant.

[ 140 ]

Marek closed the sketch pad and looked down at the cover for a few moments, then at Jessie. She was sitting quietly, staring off into space, and Wendy knew that the girl was once more experiencing what she had the other day, and Wendy remembered her interest in what Jessie had termed "her spells." Was Jessie prone to epilepsy or something similar?

Marek addressed the girl, this time in Czech.

Jessie responded, sounding frightened. He spoke to her again, obviously asking her something, and she reached out her hand and he took it and held it reassuringly. She spoke for a long time, without interruption, her eyes wide and unseeing. Finally she started crying and Marek gently shook the girl until her eyes focused again. Slowly she slid off the chair and went to Wendy, who put her arms around her.

"What did she say?" Wendy asked after a few moments when he didn't speak.

"She said her name was Ružena." He turned around so that he could look at Wendy. "My cousin—one of my many cousins who went to her death at Auschwitz—was named that. It means Rose in Czech. And she says that she is eleven years old and she is scared, because her father and uncle and older cousin have been separated from them, and she is walking behind her mother, who is going to have another baby, and her mother is holding onto her tiny sister, and her aunt holds her other sister, and her younger cousin is helping grandfather, who is ill. Another little boy and her grandmother follow behind her. Men dressed in what she thinks are pajamas are yelling, and her line is going forward, and she is so afraid that she won't see her family again. Then she says the men in uniform force them to undress in a long cold room, and she is so embarrassed because she has just become a woman and the blood is running down her leg, and the men in uniform are pointing at her and laughing. Her little cousin puts his arms around her to comfort her, and her grandmother strokes her cheek, but she says she is too humiliated to look up. Then they are told to go into the shower room, and it is dark there and the door is closed behind them, and they all begin to panic because this doesn't seem like a shower room. They are moving toward the door, trying to get out; some are shouting or screaming, others are banging on the doors with their fists, trying to open it but it has been locked from the outside, and they hear a grate or something overhead being moved, and then . . . and then . . ."

He dropped his head in his hands.

Wendy stood, holding the child against her, wanting to comfort Marek as well. She didn't know what to do. She could do too much—or not enough. She reached out and simply put her hand on his shoulder. She guessed at the pain he was feeling as he relieved those years in the camps. Memories from long ago, memories that could never be removed.

Finally, he raised his head and she saw the look in his eyes.

"She knows things—terrible things—that no American child could know," he said, his voice almost a whisper. "If her parents or grandparents had been survivors of the Holocaust, I could understand that she might know a few details. But not this. Only someone who had been there could know. And there are these as well." He indicated the sketches inside the pad. "These are far too accurate for someone who wasn't there."

"Then how does she know it?" Wendy asked. She maneuvered herself around so that she was sitting in Jessie's old chair. The girl had fallen asleep in her arms, and Wendy noticed not for the first time that the girl often slept after one of these spells. Perhaps it was too great a strain for her mind and her body. It might be her only means of escape.

"I have thought about this much since yesterday, Wendy—I couldn't sleep last night. But. You will think me crazy." He looked at her and she could see that he wanted her to believe him.

"No."

"What if?—no."

"Go on." She tried to look reassuring.

He sighed. "We know a few things . . . that she could not have seen it on TV—it's not the sort of thing a child would watch—and that no one in her family told her. We know she is not old enough to have lived through that time. So, what is left?" Wendy just watched him. "Only what can seem absurd. And yet . . . what if—somehow—the spirit of a camp victim is . . . living . . . in the little girl."

Wendy stared at him. She couldn't think of anything to say—this was surely the most preposterous thing she had ever heard. Had he hit his head hard sometime? Was he crazy?

The minutes passed as Wendy just stared at Marek. Finally, he said, "Wendy? Are you all right? Did you hear what I said?"

"I heard," she said. "But I just can't . . . it's impossible. Possession?" Her own church, the Catholic church, believed in possession

[ 142 ]

by spirits. In the modern world it was not always an acknowledged tenet, but that didn't make the belief any less real. For centuries humans had believed in possession, had created elaborate ceremonies to rid the victim of the unwelcome spirit. The Catholic Church wasn't the only one to believe in possession or whatever it was being called in these secular days.

He shook his head. "No. I don't think it can really be called possession. At least, I don't think so." He smiled briefly. "I think if it were completely possession, we would hear only from Ružena, but as it happens we have seen Ružena come out only in times of great distress for Jessie and for Ružena; all the other times the child we talk to and watch is completely Jessie. So, I think it is like two people are living there, in Jessie, at the same time. One who belongs. And one who doesn't, but who has come to this girl—from wherever—for some reason, I think. Maybe Jessie is a reincarnation of my cousin. If we cannot discount possession, then we cannot rule out reincarnation."

Reincarnation now, Wendy thought. Possession and/or reincarnation. Stefan had flipped out; she knew it. That had to be the reason he was babbling on about this nonsense.

Except that he wasn't babbling, was he? He was completely serious. He expected her to consider it, expected her to be as serious as he. And yet as incredible as it sounded, what if he was right?

Wendy's smile was ironic. "No, I suppose not, but . . . it's amazing, Stefan, you have to admit that. I mean, how did this happen—if indeed it did? And why to Jessie?" Of course, if it wasn't possession or reincarnation, what *was* the explanation? She had none.

"I don't know, but I'd like to find out. I think there must be a reason—that this is not completely an accident, you know."

"More importantly—is this dangerous for Jessie?" She was thinking of the girl's fear yesterday.

"I don't know. Do you think you can wake her? I must ask her some questions."

"I'll try." Gently she shook Jessie and called her name.

Groggily the girl answered. Wendy kept calling her name until Jessie finally opened her eyes. She didn't think the girl looked too alert, but at least she wasn't asleep any more.

"Jessie, can you hear me?" Marek asked.

She nodded. She was sitting up now, leaning back against Wendy.

[ 143 ]

"Will you please answer me, if you can?"

"Yes." Her reply was very sleepy.

"I need to know about your spells."

Wendy felt the girl's body stiffen.

"It's all right," Wendy said. "You aren't in any trouble."

The girl relaxed.

"This is very important now, Jessie," Marek said as he leaned closer. "When did your spells first begin? I must know this."

"They started when we moved here." She yawned and rubbed an eye with the heel of her hand.

"To Hunters Heights?"

"Yes."

"You didn't have these spells when you lived in Kentucky?"

"No, sir."

"Are they getting better or worse now, do you think?"

"Worse. They weren't too bad the first day or so, but then they got mighty awful on my birthday, which was last Saturday, and they've been real bad ever since."

"That's when you turned eleven, correct?"

"Yes."

He looked at Wendy. "My cousin was eleven when she died. This little girl has just turned eleven."

Wendy frowned slightly. "Why would she start having these spells or whatever they are when she comes to Hunters Heights?" Wendy wanted to know. "That sounds as if something must have triggered the spells? But what? The move? The move *here*?"

Marek tapped his fingers on the tabletop for a few minutes as he studied the girl. Jessie's eyelids were drooping again, and she looked like she was about to fall asleep again.

"I wonder if this isn't too complicated for us. Perhaps Jessie should see a psychologist or someone equally qualified to hypnotize her. Perhaps reliving that time under the hypnosis will ease the memories. Maybe you could talk with her parents about such a thing."

Wendy shook her head. "I doubt it. Honey, why don't you go check on the cats for me? They're too quiet—which means they're probably in trouble somewhere!" Jessie nodded, jumped off Wendy's lap, and headed upstairs to where she knew the cats would be curled up. "Frankly, Stefan, I think that's out of the question. Her parents are fairly unreasonable, and I suspect the stepfather is abusing her somehow, although I have no proof of that. I don't want to give him

[ 144 ]

another reason to hit or yell at her. They'd never believe a word of what we say."

"I see."

"Then what do we do? Jessie told me she was sent home from school the other day, and today she started to have a spell, but it was on her lunch break so she managed to cover it up. She's getting worried, and she told me she didn't get much sleep last night or the night before. She says she's afraid; she won't say of what, though. It's affecting her school and her life." She looked down at the sketch pad. "Why would someone . . . Ružena . . . whoever . . . come to Jessie, of all people? What could Ružena—or whoever—be trying to accomplish? If indeed, there is a purpose. There has to be one, doesn't there?" She looked earnestly at the man. She wanted to believe all that was happening to Jessie wasn't random.

"I hope," he said slowly, "that we find that out soon."

Wendy thought he was about to speak again, and she had the strangest feeling he might already know the answer. Might know it, but be unprepared to accept it or tell her. And she could hear the unspoken words: *before it's too late.*


Dr. Emerson Thorne smiled at his last patient of the afternoon—he had an abbreviated day today—a seven-year-old boy who had just had the cast on his arm removed, and watched as the child and his mother left the office.

As soon as the door closed, the smile slid from his face. He sat back down in his desk chair and swiveled so that he could look out the window.

Once more he played over the events of the previous afternoon. He had heard Jessica call him by his old name. He was convinced.

He knew it for a fact. Yes, yes, he did.

He tapped his gold-plated pen against the blotter and stared off into space.

When he had asked what she wanted of him, she had addressed him by the name, plain as day. He had heard it so very clearly.

The old name that he hadn't used in so long.

He had almost forgotten it.

Almost.

And now she had whispered it aloud, said it so that it was in the open once more. It had hung in the air between them.

He frowned and set the pen down carefully at a right angle to the blotter. He folded his hands together and studied his manicured nails. The frown deepened.

This was not a good thing, he knew. Because if she knew . . . who else might know? Her parents? The neighbor? Her school?

No; that was crazy thinking. The girl knew, and she had not told anyone. She was too frightened to do so.

So far.

But she would doubtless tell someone eventually.

Which was why, he decided as he stood, he must do something about her.

Tonight.

He would visit the child who knew too much.

Tomorrow he would be free again.

# TWENTY-FIVE

Wendy pushed the cart without looking where she was going. Marek had left about an hour ago, and Wendy remembered she needed to pick up some items at the Tri-Mart, a big discount department store outside of town; it was mostly stuff for her office, and so she asked Jessie if she'd like to come along.

Jessie had nodded vigorously. Wendy had insisted on calling Astrid first, though, and asking if it were all right, and Jessie's mother, who had sounded like she had been napping, had said in a slurred voice that she didn't mind as long as she was back home by seven.

Wendy got the distinct impression that Astrid didn't much care where her daughter was, as long as it wasn't in her house. Right now Jessie was off in another aisle, hunting for rolls of paper towels; the store was having a sale on a certain brand, and they were far cheaper than at the supermarket.

As Wendy went down the office-supply aisle, she heard a distinct thunk.

Oh God, I've probably knocked over some end display and made a mess. When she looked up, though, she saw that she had simply run into another cart.

Car or cart, she was doing too much of that recently, she decided.

"I'm sorry," she began, then realized who she had run into. "Dr. Thorne! I'm sorry. I wasn't watching where I was going."

"That's quite all right, my dear. No damage done."

"Good. Again, I'm really sorry. I should be watching more."

"You look like your mind was on other matters, far more important than typing paper."

"It is, I guess."

His look of concern deepened.

"It's my young neighbor," she confided.

"She's not sick again, is she?"

She shook her head. "No, no, she's not. It's . . . well, she's been acting odd . . . oh, I don't know . . . ," she shrugged, "it's kind of hard to explain. It's all very weird."

"Perhaps talking to someone—a medical professional—might help?" He was looking at her, not blinking.

"It might. Maybe we can get together some time in the diner and talk about it. I don't know what to do."

"I would like to have dinner with you very much. Just let me know when."

"I guess I ought to be going. Jessie's around here some place, and I should get home and start dinner and see that she gets home in time for hers."

"The girl is here?" he asked casually.

Wendy waved a hand. "I gave her a list of things to fetch to help me. We'll be meeting up someplace."

He bowed slightly. "Until then, Miss Wallace. Good day." He pushed his cart away.

Wendy smiled after him, set several reams of typing paper and a few ballpoint pens in the basket, and began searching for Jessie. It occurred to her that she was running into a lot of people at the store. Well, two, she corrected mentally.

Marek and Thorne.

For some reason that made her frown.

Jessie rounded the far end of the office-supply aisle and stopped dead in her tracks. At the opposite end stood Wendy, and she was talking with the doctor.

Jessie swallowed. She could feel things beginning to get gray and weird around her, and she forced herself not to lose consciousness. Not now, not when he was so close to her. She had to be awake, had to be alert. She heard a pounding or roaring in her ears, heard the faint shrieks of those people.

She shook her head. No, no, no.

What could Wendy have to say to him? Maybe he had stopped to ask Wendy how Jessie was doing? No, that was stupid. They were both acting too friendly. Wendy was friends with this man? No! she wanted to scream, but she couldn't deny the way the woman smiled at the doctor.

[ 148 ]

Jessie watched as he bowed slightly and walked away. She waited until she couldn't see him any more and then she went in the opposite direction, down that aisle and around to find Wendy.

"Hi there. Got all the items?" Jessie nodded and placed the paper towels in the basket. "Good. I think that about does it. I'm ready to go."

Wendy headed toward a checkout and Jessie trailed. She kept looking behind her, but didn't see him. She didn't want him to see her.

"You okay?" Wendy asked as she started putting items on the belt.

"Sure." Jessie moved closer to help, then went around to the front of the counter so she could start bagging. All the while she kept an eye open. She didn't see him. Where was he? she wondered. Could he have already left? What if he were out in the parking lot, waiting for her to come out? She wouldn't know until she stepped outside if the silver Mercedes were there.

What if he tried to hurt her and somehow hurt Wendy? Or what if— She looked at Wendy, who was busy writing out a check.

What if Wendy and the man were . . . talking . . . talking about her? What if Wendy wasn't really her friend, but his, and what if—

Jessie stopped this line of thinking. She couldn't stand to consider it.

She didn't speak much on the short drive back to Wendy's house and she knew that the woman glanced over at her several times. She didn't say a word; she couldn't think of anything to say.

When they pulled into Wendy's driveway and the car came to a stop, Jessie opened the door.

"I better go home."

"All right, Jessie." She paused, then: "Is there anything wrong?"

"Wrong?" Jessie tried to sound like she didn't know what the woman meant. She didn't want to talk to Wendy, not now.

"Is there anything you want to talk about?"

Jessie couldn't meet Wendy's eyes as she lied. "No, nothin'."

"All right, Jessie. See you later then?"

Jessie nodded and slipped out of the car and shut the door, then walked across to her house. She didn't look back. She went inside, past her mother, who was napping on the downstairs couch, and upstairs to her room. She sat by the window and stared down as Wendy took her purchases into her house.

The phone rang and she ran to get it; she didn't want her

mother to be disturbed, although usually it took a lot more than a ringing phone to wake her.

"Hello?"

"It's me." Patrick.

"Yeah?"

"What do you mean 'yeah'?" he demanded.

She said nothing.

"Are you there?"

"Yes." She knew better than to say "yeah" again.

"I wanna talk to your mother."

"She's napping."

"Wake her up."

"I'll take a message for her."

"You will, will you? Tell her, Jess, that I'll be home a bit early and dinner better be on the table."

She made a face at the handset. "Is that all?"

"No, it's not. I got a little message for you, missy."

She waited.

"You better start acting nicer to your old dad than you have been."

"You're not my father," she replied.

"I'm the only father you've got now that your old man managed to get himself killed. And another thing, kiddo—your mom didn't want you to know this, but I think it's about time for you to learn that your sainted father wasn't quite as perfect as you thought he was. He was havin' an affair with some broad from work, and he was planning on moving in with her and her kid. He was gonna abandon your mom and *you*, Jess. How ya like them apples?"

Jessie looked at the handset. "It's not true," she said, but her voice was wobbly. She didn't want to believe him, but there was something about his voice, something that made her suspect he told the truth. Patrick never told the truth, did he?

"Sure is. Ask your mother. When she hasn't been drinking, that is. Your dad wasn't killed comin' back from the store, by the way; he was heading on over to his bimbo's place with some of his stuff when he got creamed." He laughed shortly. "And here you thought you were his golden-haired angel."

Jessie slammed down the phone. It rang again and she lifted the handset, quickly pressed down on the cradle to disconnect, and then dropped the handset on the table. There. No one could call now.

[ 150 ]

She found her way back to her room and sank onto her bed. No one could call and tell her hurtful lies like that now. No one.

She wanted to deny what Patrick had said, but she was so afraid that he was telling the truth. She wanted to cry, but for some reason she couldn't. She remembered so many nights when her father and mother had argued, and the shouting had kept her awake. She remembered her mother screaming some woman's name. Not just any woman's name, though.

She squeezed her eyes shut.

Her father had betrayed her and her love for him. She felt all shriveled up inside and cold, even though it was a warm day. She looked across at Wendy's house and thought about Wendy talking to the doctor, being friends with the man who wanted to kill her. She swallowed heavily.

More betrayal.

She couldn't sit here and wait to see what happened with the doctor or Wendy—or her stepfather. She had to do something.

She was a very well read child, and she knew precisely what someone needed on a venture like this. After all, she had been camping, too.

She took out her knapsack and put some clean underwear in it and extra socks, as well as a fresh blouse and shorts. She changed into jeans and a long-sleeved shirt and sturdy shoes. She looked around her room. She selected two pads of paper and put her pencils and eraser into a pouch, then into the knapsack. She also put in her new jacket. She located the flashlight that her mother kept in the linen closet upstairs in case the electricity should go off, and deposited it with her other things.

She left the knapsack in her room and went downstairs quietly so as not to disturb her mother, who was still asleep. She slipped into the kitchen and peered into the cupboards and refrigerator to see what she could find. She found a paper bag and put some apples and some boxes of raisins in it, then went to where her mother kept her purse and opened it, looking around to make sure that her mother couldn't see her. She found a ten-dollar bill and a handful of fives. Jessie slipped three of the fives into a hip pocket. She felt bad about taking her mother's money, but she had to have some. She also took a handful of matchbooks. She didn't know if she would need them, but better safe than sorry, as her father had always told her.

Her father. Her face wrinkled up.

[ 151 ]

She looked around the kitchen some more to see what else she should take. She found a ball of twine and a steak knife.

Upstairs again, she emptied out her piggy bank, took all the quarters and dollar bills, and left the small change in a pool of silver and copper on her bed. She put the stuffed cat from her dresser in her knapsack.

She took one last glance around her room, then closed the door and went downstairs. It was close to dusk now. Good. She wouldn't be noticed as much. She had changed into dark colors; she didn't want to stand out.

She paused in the living room and stared down at her mother, who was still asleep. Astrid was having a bad dream, Jessie guessed, because tears were flowing from under her closed eyelids. Jessie bent down and gently kissed her forehead.

She remembered how years ago, when her father was still alive, she and her parents had gone to an amusement park, and they had ridden all the rides and eaten cotton candy and drunk cup after cup of lemonade, and when they had come home, her mother had collapsed onto the couch with a sigh and promptly fallen asleep, and after a while had begun to gently snore. She and her father had giggled at what would be their own special secret.

Tears blurred her eyes, and she wiped at them with the back of her hand.

She had thought about leaving a note, but she didn't know what to say. It would be hours before her mother and Patrick suspected anything wrong. At first her mother would just think she was next door, and Jessie would be long gone before Astrid thought to call. Where would she leave a note, anyway? It just might tip them off faster if she did leave one.

Long gone. She shivered.

She left the house and cut across the back of Wendy's lawn. She didn't want to go down the street; *he* might be waiting there.

Dudley was out, digging a hole by the gazebo, and he let out a gentle woof when he saw her. She bent down to pet him and say good-bye—her eyes filled with tears as she thought how much she would miss him—then started walking. When she glanced back, he was following.

"Go home, Dudley," she said in her crossest voice, but the dog merely cocked his head and continued trailing after her. She stopped and pushed him back toward his yard, but he thought she was playing and wrestled with her. She patted his head and told him he could come with her, if he wanted.

She cut through neighbors' back yards, making sure she didn't see anyone, and headed toward the convenience store around the corner. Dudley followed her inside, even though she told him he would have to wait outside, but the cashier didn't seem to mind. The guy just said she had a cute dog. Jessie thanked him, and proceeded to buy some peanut butter and crackers, a loaf of raisin bread, which her mother never bought, some beef jerky—she had seen once in a Western how a guy lost in the desert for days had had nothing to eat but jerky and it had saved his life—two six-packs of soda, some Hostess cupcakes, and a box of dog biscuits for Dudley.

She put everything into her knapsack and slung it over her shoulders. It was getting kind of heavy now, but she could still manage.

"C'mon," she said to the dog.

She paid the cashier, put the change in her pocket and headed down the street. She had seen enough. She and Dudley were leaving town. She didn't know where.

She just knew she had to get away from Thorne—and from Wendy.

# TWENTY-SIX

Wendy finished typing a scene and got up to stretch. She hadn't been able to work much since coming home because mostly she'd been thinking about Jessie's odd behavior. Jessie had never been that quiet, that remote with her, and Wendy wondered what had happened. The girl hadn't been that way when they got to the store.

Could something have happened while they were there? But what?

It was a puzzle she couldn't figure out.

She glanced out into the backyard. She couldn't see Dudley at the moment, but wasn't particularly worried. He never strayed from the yard. She'd let him stay out for a bit longer, and then she'd call him in. He'd probably discovered something to dig in, something muddy to track into the house.

She smiled and returned to her work.

Thorne sat in the Mercedes up the street and waited for night to come. He glanced at the clock on the dashboard as the strains of Mozart's *Jupiter* Symphony played on the radio. He hummed along. He felt very, very good. It wouldn't be long.

And then he would take care of the little girl.

Tonight, it would be over.

No more demons from the past; no more demons to disturb his work or his sleep at night.

He stroked the oily metal of the .38 on the car seat beside him.

After tonight, he wouldn't have to worry about a single thing.

Marek frowned. He had lost track of Thorne after the man had left the Tri-Mart. Like an amateur. Thorne had gone this way, then that, and the next thing Marek knew, he couldn't locate him.

Thorne left the store just minutes after Wendy and Jessie had left it.

Another curious matter, Marek thought.

Was Thorne meeting her there? What was it with those two?

He decided that he had to know, had to find out from her tonight.

He had to find Thorne. Fast.

"Oh, Patrick honey, would you call Jessica? She's next door at Miz Wallace's." Astrid was busy cooking and didn't look up, so she missed her husband's frown.

Patrick sighed deeply, as if she were asking the most impossible task of him. Astrid still didn't look up at the sound, so he went to the back door and stepped out onto the porch. He supposed that the girl hadn't said anything about his phone call, since Astrid hadn't mentioned it to him. When he got home, he had found the upstairs receiver off the hook, though.

"Jessica!" he bellowed. "Jessica! Come home! Time for dinner!"

He strolled back in, letting the screen door slam shut, which always made Astrid wince, and then got a can of beer from the refrigerator, opened it, settled at the table, and watched his wife; it never occurred to him to offer any help. Astrid popped the chicken into the oven, washed her hands, and dried them.

She glanced at the clock. "I said for her to be home by seven, and here it is ten minutes past." She went to the door and called Jessie's name. When the girl didn't come out of Wendy's house, Astrid frowned. "I'll be right back, honey."

"Sure," Patrick said as he took a swig of beer.

Astrid slowly stepped across the driveway to Wendy's back door. She felt very strange doing this. She hadn't talked with her neighbor much, and perhaps she should have. She just couldn't bring herself to. She had a feeling that Wendy Wallace didn't approve of her. Besides, Wendy seemed to be doing better at being a mother to Jessie than she did, and Astrid was more than a little embarrassed—and hurt—by that.

She knocked on the screen door and waited. A few moments later Wendy came into the kitchen.

"Mrs. Fields, hi." She unlatched the door and opened it, but Astrid remained where she was.

She put on her most social expression. "Good evenin', Miz

Wallace. I was wonderin' if you could send my daughter home. It's nearly time for dinner."

"Oh, I'm sorry, Mrs. Fields, but Jessie went home hours ago. We went to the store this afternoon, and when we came back she went right home."

Astrid blinked. "Are you sure?"

"Quite. I saw her go into the house."

"Oh, well, I'm sorry to bother you then. She's just so quiet sometimes that I seem to misplace her." Astrid laughed, a nervous sound.

"Sure." Wendy smiled.

Astrid went back into her house and looked at Patrick, who was working on his second beer. Beer was so—lower class, she thought, wrinkling her nose. Her father had never approved of beer drinking; it was, he always alleged, for the working classes.

"Honey, could you go check up in Jessica's room? Miz Wallace said she came back hours ago."

Patrick rolled his eyes. "Jeez, do I have to do everything around here?"

It was on the tip of Astrid's tongue to say it would be nice if he did *something* around here, but at the last moment she decided against it. It wouldn't help, after all. He would simply snap at her, and she would snap back, and then they would fight and nothing would be accomplished. He would drink more beer, and she would get a headache and have to go lie down.

No wonder Jessica spent so much time next door. She imagined that Wendy didn't get headaches and yell.

"Patrick, please," she said, mustering her sweetest tone.

He glanced up at her, then pushed back his chair with a scraping noise that made her clench her teeth. He belched, then headed upstairs.

Astrid checked on the potatoes and saw they were coming along quite well; she checked on the chicken. She inhaled deeply; she always loved tarragon on chicken.

Minutes passed, and still Patrick wasn't back. She hoped he wasn't nagging Jessica. She really was a good little girl.

Finally, he came downstairs. He had a strange expression on his face.

Ice clutched at Astrid's heart, and she gripped the back of a chair for support. "What's wrong?"

"She's not there."

"Don't be silly. She's got to be there. She's not next door, and she's not out in the backyard." Astrid pushed past him and went upstairs to her daughter's room, but when she saw the pennies and nickels on the bed, the open closet where several pieces of clothing had fallen to the floor, the one dresser drawer that wasn't closed because a sock stuck out of it, and the missing stuffed animal, she knew something had happened. Jessica would never leave her room looking like this. She was always particular about how it looked.

And if Jessica Mae were not next door, and if she weren't in the backyard, and if she weren't in her room—Astrid rushed into her room.

No child.

Astrid searched all the rooms upstairs.

Not a sign of her daughter.

"Jessica's run away!" she said. As Patrick came up behind her, she dropped her face into her hands and began sobbing.

# TWENTY-SEVEN

Jessie had walked for what seemed liked hours now, and the sun was going down, and she was getting tired and really had to go to the bathroom. Dudley followed patiently behind her.

Once before they'd left town they had stopped so he could drink some water from someone's sprinklers. He had gotten all wet, and then he shook himself and sprinkled her with droplets, and she had giggled. He had barked in response.

She had headed out of town and was walking along the highway now. The farther away from Hunters Heights she went the better she felt; she didn't think her spells would come back now. She saw a gas station up ahead and wondered if she could use its bathroom.

She asked, and the guy who looked at her sweaty face nodded and handed her the key, attached to a big wooden block. She went around the side and unlocked the door; Dudley came in with her, and Jessie made sure she locked the bathroom door.

She wrinkled her nose at what she saw. It wasn't as nicely kept as her mother's bathroom, but on the other hand, at least it wasn't a privy. She had seen—and used—enough of those when she lived down south.

She took her time; she didn't know when she would be able to go inside again. When she was finished, she flushed the toilet and washed her hands, carefully drying them on a paper towel. She grabbed a handful of them and stuck them into her knapsack, then she cupped her hands under the running cold water and drank long. She plugged up the sink and with a slight grunt lifted Dudley so he could have a drink too. She let him lap up as much as he wanted; they both needed the water.

She wanted to make her sodas last; she didn't know how long she and Dudley would be . . . wherever. She should have packed a

Thermos and then kept filling it with water. She shrugged. Well, she couldn't think of everything, could she?

She returned the key to the man and thanked him, then bought a map of New Jersey from him and a candy bar from the machine. As she walked along, she ate half of it, then gave the rest to the dog, who gobbled it down. She stopped by the road some distance away from the gas station, sat on a fallen log, and opened the map.

Here was Hunters Heights, and here she was, she realized, looking back at the road sign opposite the gas station and then down at the map where the same number appeared. It looked like she'd come three or four miles. Not very far, she thought.

She had to decide where she was going. She couldn't just aimlessly walk along the road in plain view of everyone. Eventually her mother would figure out she was gone and she'd call the police and they would start searching for her. The first place the police would look for her would be along major roads, such as this one.

"Not good, Dudley," she said aloud.

He cocked his head, but didn't answer.

She squinted as she peered around. Mostly woods up ahead, to the sides and back of her. There weren't many options. She could strike out through the woods . . . but she'd have to watch out for poison ivy and snakes and such.

She told herself she was being a baby. The snakes wouldn't bother her if she didn't bother them. She couldn't avoid the woods. Not really. The area was thick with them. Maybe that would be a better cover; no one could see her in the midst of all the trees and bushes and vines.

But wait, here was a small road, a thin black line. She looked at the legend, as they had taught her in school, and she saw that the black line meant an insignificant route, completely undeveloped. No one would think to search for her there. Maybe it was some old mining road; there were miles and miles of them around here, she knew, never used any more. The mines had given out long ago, and the roads had probably been reclaimed by nature.

Better and better, she told herself.

Carefully she folded the map, realized she'd done it wrong, and had to start all over again. Then she tucked it into her knapsack.

"I should have found some saddlebags for you, Dud," she said as she scratched his head. "Then you could have carried more. I could have packed us some sandwiches"—she thought longingly of the lunch meat her mother always had on hand—"and a Thermos or two, and some more dog food, and maybe a blanket." She patted his head while he panted. "Maybe it would have been better if you were a pack pony; you could carry more. C'mon."

She stood and dusted the back of her jeans. She spotted a straight branch lying not far away and picked it up. It was almost as tall as she was, and the bark had fallen off in long strips so that most of the wood underneath showed through. It would make a nice walking stick, and didn't people who went traveling or hiking always have sticks like this?

She was going to have to figure out what she planned on doing, and real soon. Even sooner than that she'd have to find a place to spend the night.

She sighed. Maybe she hadn't planned this thing as well as she'd thought. It was too late, though, to go back. Besides, what would she be returning to? The doctor? Wendy's friendship? Her father's betrayal?

Tears clouded her eyes and she started walking again, the dog following her. When she came to the road she'd found on the map, she turned onto it, and never looked back toward the main road.

Thorne watched as night fell. Lights had come on gradually all over the neighborhood; there seemed to be more lights than usual switched on at the Fieldses' house. It looked like just about every room there had a light on in it, which he found odd.

It would be some time before the lights were off and the occupants were asleep. He knew which bedroom the parents slept in; he knew where the little girl's room was located. He had stood under her window at night often enough to know that.

He would have to wait; that was all right, he was a patient man.

Suddenly he saw a police car roll into the Fieldses' driveway and a uniformed cop get out. Thorne frowned. What was going on?

Minutes later a second patrol car pulled up. He sat up and peered more closely. Of course, he couldn't hear anything from this distance, but he could drive by perhaps and see what was happening.

He switched on the ignition, turned the headlights on and drove slowly down the street. He braked slightly and glanced in through the front window of the Fieldses' house. He could see the mother sobbing and trying to talk; the stepfather had his arm around the woman, and one of the cops was writing something down on a pad of paper.

Something had happened. To the girl.

Thorne frowned as he drove past the house; he turned around in a driveway some houses down and went by again. The same scene was being played out.

What could have happened? What would have prompted the police to visit the parents?

There could only be two possibilities: that the girl had had an accident or gotten into some trouble; or more likely, that she had seen him talking to the Wallace woman in the store and had run away.

He cursed in German under his breath. He slammed his hand against the steering wheel and parked on the street a few houses away. The little bitch!

What rotten luck.

Unless, he thought as he looked in his rearview mirror, he found her first.

# TWENTY-EIGHT

Jessie saw a raccoon waddling down the road. Dudley barked at the animal, and she hushed him. The raccoon looked back over its shoulder and then went loping off into the bushes.

She decided it was time to leave the road too. The moon wasn't out yet, and it was pretty dark, but she had taken out her flashlight, and she would shine it ahead of her ever so often to make sure the path was still clear. She needed to find some place to spend the night real soon. Maybe an abandoned cabin or a cave. Something like that.

As she moved away from the road she nearly tripped over some rails and she knew these must have been used for an iron mine nearby. The rails were long rusted, and the wooden ties were rotting.

She was getting pretty tired, too, and as she rubbed the back of her stiff neck, she realized with rising panic that her chain and her father's ring were missing. She felt for it, in case it had slipped down inside her shirt, but it was gone. She flashed the light back the way she had come, but nothing glinted.

The ring was gone, and she felt like crying, even though, she told herself, it was just her dad's ring. It wasn't important to her any more, and for some reason that made her want to cry even more.

Dudley bounced toward her and growled, almost as if he were warning her away from stepping forward, and when she shone the flashlight on the ground ahead of her, she saw a pit filled with boulders and logs and stumps. Most of the vegetation was rotting now, and the pit was a good fifteen or twenty feet deep.

She had almost fallen into that, too. She had to be more careful. If she fell and hurt herself out here, no one would find her. Ever. She'd die of starvation and her body would rot and the bones would bleach, and she'd be all alone.

She took a deep breath and took a step away from the mining pit.

Suddenly Dudley darted off one way. Impatiently Jessie called to him, but he didn't return.

"Darned dog," she muttered, and tramped after him. It was up to her to watch after him; she didn't want him hurt. Wendy would get awfully mad at her if something happened to the dog, and she didn't want that. It didn't matter that she didn't think she would ever see—or talk to—Wendy again.

Dudley was beneath an oak tree, gazing upward intently and barking. Jessie turned the flashlight's beam on the foliage and saw two pairs of yellow eyes staring back at her.

"Good, Dud. You found some kitties. C'mon." She turned around and the dog obediently trotted after her. She didn't know how far off the road she was; hard to say in the dark. In the morning, she'd be able to tell where she was. She hoped. Should have packed a compass, she told herself with a slight sigh. She would have to start making a list of things to take when she ran away . . . the next time. She almost giggled aloud.

Jessie flashed the light ahead and saw something dark beyond some bushes. She tentatively poked the bushes with her walking stick. An opening lay beyond. She shone the light in and saw a large steel plate lying on the ground. She thought it had once covered the opening, which had to lead to one of the iron mines, but somehow it had come off; maybe someone had camped here before. She pushed her way through the chest-high bushes into the mine and looked around.

The tunnel extended back for a number of yards, but stopped with what looked liked a cave-in; there was a branch to the right. She stepped farther in, so that she could peer down the right-hand tunnel. She didn't see anything—meaning she didn't spot a hungry bear or a bobcat, all of which were common enough in this area yet—about to pounce on her. The people hadn't managed to drive all the wildlife out yet.

She took a deep breath, but didn't detect anything rank. Her dad had always said you could tell when a bear was nearby—you could smell it. She swallowed heavily. The air smelled mostly like wet leaves and dust.

She heard a faint dripping sound and walked toward it. The flashlight caught a pool of water. Dudley bounded past her and began lapping at it.

"Stop it!" she yelled. She didn't know if the water was good; what if it was poisoned or something? She tried to pull Dudley away, but he was too thirsty.

Finally, he looked up at her, water dripping off his muzzle. She could see now that water trickled from a small opening in the ceiling of this secondary tunnel, and it had formed a shallow pool on the ground.

She peered at Dudley, who gazed back at her. He didn't seem sick. She cupped one hand and held it under the trickling water, then held her hand to her mouth. The water tasted kind of like iron, but beyond that it seemed okay.

"You can go ahead and drink there again," she said, but sternly, to let the dog know that she didn't approve of him rushing off and doing things before she could check them through first.

Dudley simply wagged his tail.

She walked back toward the opening, and this time found a niche along one side of the tunnel some distance from the entrance.

She realized she could easily fit in the nook, with her knapsack and Dudley, and still have room left over, and she would be hidden as well. It looked pretty cozy, and she had to admit she was pretty tired. It had been a long day, and she hadn't walked that much since her dad and she had gone on hikes.

She wondered why it was there and guessed the miners must have stored equipment in it at one time.

She sat inside the niche and leaned her head against the wall, and Dudley crawled into her lap. She stroked his head. She had turned off the flashlight to save the battery and now she saw just how dark it was. She could hear crackling noises outside the mine, and a hooting from high up, which she knew was an owl. There were other sounds, though, that she couldn't identify, and that bothered her.

Jessie had never been afraid of the dark—when she was in her own room. Now—out here, out in the open, on her own, with no one else around for miles and miles—that was something else.

She didn't think she would be able to sleep now, despite being exhausted. Something—or someone—might come creeping up on her. No, she had a watchdog who would keep guard and protect her from anything—anyone—who came in here. A gentle snoring rose from her lap; the dog was already asleep.

She grinned. Some watchdog.

Maybe she should start a small fire. Something big enough to keep her warm—and to give off light. It would scare away any animals that might come hunting for a girl-size meal, too. And it would reassure her; the mine wouldn't be pitch-black then.

But the fire might also attract humans.

She would have to take the chance. She couldn't sit here in the dark all night long.

She eased out of the niche. Dudley yawned and blinked, and she told him to go back to sleep. She left her knapsack with the dog and, taking the flashlight, went to the front of the mine and began poking through the underbrush. She needed some wood.

She dragged a number of branches back to the mouth of the mine and stacked them, then found some twigs. She shut off her flashlight again and dragged the firewood to an area near the niche. She didn't want it too close to her, but close enough that she would keep warm.

She was getting thirsty again, so she paused to drink more water. She hoped it was okay. Dudley had been drinking more, and he seemed all right. That had to be a good sign.

She arranged the wood as her father had taught her, then went looking for more branches which she stacked beyond the niche. Wood for later on, when the flames began to burn down. She bet she had enough for all night. If she were going to stay here the next night, she'd have to go out and search for more wood during the day. She would have to be careful, too, because they would probably have people out looking for her by then.

She peered at the stack. Was that enough? Or should she get more? More, she decided.

She hunted around for additional branches and twigs. Once she heard something moving through the fallen leaves, and she paused, holding her breath. A moment later it squeaked, and she knew it was just some animal, one that wouldn't hurt her.

She dragged the wood back to the mine; she also found some large pieces of bark which she knew would burn well. Dudley had awakened by now and had followed her out, then followed her back inside.

She stacked the new branches, dusted her hands, then went to the entrance and tried to lift the steel plate. Maybe she could prop it up, so the opening would be partially closed. However, the plate was too heavy for her to lift, much less drag; she wondered what had knocked it down in the first place.

Must have been big. Real big. She hoped it wasn't around any more.

"Stand back, Dudley." He did so.

She turned on her flashlight, set it on the dirt floor, and took the paper towels out of her knapsack. She twisted and balled them, as her father had told her to do with kindling, and stuck some twigs into the paper, and put them under the bigger wood. Then she took out a book of matches and struck one.

The match flickered and the dog barked, and she shushed him. She lit the paper and watched as the flame spread along it to the twigs, and then to the wood. She watched as the fire spread along the wood. She wouldn't need any more matches.

She had her fire.

She settled back into her niche, took out her jacket and put it across her front. Dudley crawled underneath into her arms, and as Jessie looked at the flames, she wondered what time it was, wondered what her mother was doing, and she began crying.

# TWENTY-NINE

Marek pulled into the driveway, slammed on the brakes, and jumped out. He glanced briefly next door at the two police cars and wondered what was going on. He walked around to the back of Wendy's house, and knocked just as she was coming to the screen.

"Stefan, thank God, you're here!" Wendy began, the same time he asked, "What's this about you and Dr. Thorne meeting?"

They stared at one another, Marek frowning. Wendy looked puzzled.

"What? What do you mean?" She opened the door and let him in. He walked into the kitchen and leaned against one of the cabinets. "You go first."

"No, you." His scowl had deepened. "What's going on next door?"

Wendy's words tumbled out. "I went to call Dudley in, and he didn't respond, and I haven't been able to find him even though I've looked all over the neighborhood, and I went next door to see if they might have seen him, and that's when I found out that Jessie is gone, and her parents think she's run away. The police were just over here to talk to me, since it seems I was the last person to have seen her this afternoon." She was wringing her hands, something she obviously didn't want to do; occasionally she would realize what she was doing and force them apart.

"Jessie doesn't seem like the type of child to run away."

"I know. That's what I said to the police."

Wendy had stepped into the darkened living room so she could watch the other house and the activity there.

"I don't understand it, Stefan. Jessie wasn't upset when she went home." She stopped. "Wait a minute." She whirled to face him. "We went to the store after you left, and while we were there she started acting kind of peculiar. She didn't talk at all on the way home, which is pretty unusual for her, and when we got back here, she just jumped out and said she had to go. I didn't think much about it at the time, but looking back now I see that was really out of character for her."

"Did something happen at the store?" Still scowling, he was staring out at the street now. A light-colored car drove by at a reduced speed, and his frown increased. It would be interesting if she didn't mention her meeting with the doctor.

"No, nothing. She got some sale items for me. Oh yeah, and I ran into Dr. Thorne."

"You did?" He was surprised she mentioned it. It wasn't what he expected.

"Yes, and I had the funniest feeling he had done it deliberately. You know, rather like when you ran into me at the supermarket the other day."

Wendy was looking at him frankly now, and Marek realized that his suspicions of her had been absurd. This woman was not colluding with the doctor; he had known that from the beginning, but he would bend over backward not to be too trusting. After all, he had been hurt too many times before. He liked this woman—wanted to like her even more—but one part of him remained forever suspicious, even in the face of her innocence.

He spread his hands. "It's true, Wendy. I ran into you deliberately there. I had been following you."

"What about our car accident?"

"That was indeed by chance. Believe me, I was not at all happy about that encounter." He was watching the street once more.

"Who are you looking for?" she demanded. "Every time we're together you're looking for someone or something. What's going on with you? Why the hell were you following me?" For the first time she noticed that he had brought in an attaché case. "What's in that?"

She sounded very suspicious now, and he didn't blame her at all.

"So many questions," he said, trying to make his voice light, but he could see even in the darkness that she was in no mood to be humored. "Well, what question do I answer first?"

"Try starting with why you were following me the other day."

"I followed you because I had seen you with a certain person. I have been watching a particular person."

[ 168 ]

"Who?"

He shrugged.

"Stefan. Come on."

He swung around to her. "All right. I have been watching Dr. Thorne."

"Thorne! Why?"

Marek stared at her, at the curve of her cheek in the light from the brilliantly lit house next door, and wondered if he could trust her. The child had trusted her, had she not?

"Dr. Thorne was a Nazi doctor."

"What!" She looked astonished. "You've got to be mistaken, Stefan. Dr. Thorne is one of the county's—the state's!—most respected physicians. He's about to receive some incredible humanitarian award on Saturday; he's dined at the White House, known umpty-eleven governors and senators, for God's sake!"

Marek's voice was so low she had to bend slightly forward to hear him. "Don't you think I don't know that? That doesn't prevent him from being a wanted Nazi criminal, you know. After the war, he fled first to Switzerland, then to South America, as so many of them did—but he was very clever, this one, and he wasn't satisfied living there. Years ago he made his way up here with a new identity and background. He started a family, he became ensconced, the very symbol of respectability. However, there was an old woman here who had survived the camps, and she thought she recognized him. She talked to my uncle, and shortly after that the old lady was found dead. It was ruled an accidental death, but I know it wasn't."

"My God. It wasn't—"

"Yes, it was your Mrs. Gottlieb. My uncle contacted me, and I began doing my paperwork. Then I came to Hunters Heights. Here." He pulled open the attaché case and handed several manila folders and envelopes to her. She stepped into the kitchen so that she could read and opened them, carefully sifting through the newspaper articles, the old photographs, following the circuitous paper trail Marek had created.

He knew she didn't believe completely; how could she? She had not been in Auschwitz; she had not seen the doctor there.

It was nearly half an hour later before she returned to the darkened living room and handed the folders back to Marek. "I don't understand . . . why are you here to watch him, Stefan? I thought you were a journalist."

"I *am* a journalist. But I also hunt for Nazis. I have a—vested—

interest in this, you might say. Thorne was one of the doctors at Auschwitz. This is the man who sent my family to the ovens."

"Oh my God." She put her hand on his arm. "I didn't realize—"

He shrugged. "How could you?" He glanced out at the street, then back at Wendy. "Believe me, I have been very careful in tracing this man. This is not an accusation to be made lightly; I *know* it is him."

"I believe you." She took a deep breath. "Then when you do confront him, you'll take him to Israel for trial, like they did with Eichmann, right?"

He stared at her.

"Right, Stefan?"

He couldn't lie to her, not now.

"No," Marek said softly, "I will not take him to Israel for trial. When I finally face Dr. Thorne, I will kill him."

# THIRTY

"What?" She didn't think she had heard him correctly.

Marek gazed at her, and she thought his expression was almost a sad one.

"I think you heard me, Wendy; I just don't think you truly want to believe it."

She spun away from him, walked to the opposite side of the room. She could still see him, though, darkly outlined in the light coming from next door.

"I don't understand, Stefan. I thought you wanted justice done."

"Justice will be done."

"What kind of justice?" she insisted.

"My justice."

"No! The law doesn't work that way. Thorne should be charged, and extradited to Israel or wherever, and he should stand trial, and if he's found guilty, he'll go to prison or be executed."

"And if he gets off, do you think justice will have been served?"

"I'm talking about giving him a fair trial."

"He didn't give the children in Auschwitz a fair trial."

"You can't stand as judge, jury, and executioner."

"Why not?"

"It's not right."

"An eye for an eye," Marek said softly. "He has to pay for his crimes, crimes committed against thousands of innocent people, crimes against mankind."

"That's a biblical law. That wouldn't hold up in a court of law."

"He's not going to a court of law."

"But who appointed you to do this?" Her voice was almost a whisper.

"I did. And the ghosts of my father and mother and brothers

and grandparents and cousins, and all the others who died in that camp."

"Ghosts are talking to you now?"

"They've never stopped—not in thirty years."

"I'm sorry. I shouldn't be so flippant." Was it so impossible, after all, that ghosts might speak to someone over the distance of the years? Was this not almost the situation with Jessie—and Ružena, if indeed it was Ružena? What if Marek's young cousin had indeed come to Jessie so that justice might be served, justice for the one who had killed her and the rest of her family?

But what Marek proposed was against everything Wendy believed in. Yet how would she feel if her entire family were wiped out and one of the men who had committed the killing walked away to build a new and better life? How would she feel after all these years, to see this man being honored now as a humanitarian, for God's sake? A man who had overseen the murders of countless thousands of people.

This smacked of vigilantism, though, and she said so.

"So what," he replied. Almost sounding weary, he added, "I am about to execute a criminal, a monster, if you will."

"Doesn't this make you just as bad as him? To take someone's life?"

"I don't do this lightly. I don't do it like *him*, because of someone's politics or religion, or for the way he wears his hair, or for his sexual preference. I do it because he must be killed so that he can harm no others."

"He's an old man."

"Old men commit crimes. It is not the special province of the young."

"Maybe he shouldn't be made to pay for something that happened thirty years—half a lifetime—ago."

"The people he sent to the ovens never had the chance for those thirty years."

She knew she couldn't convince him not to kill Thorne; Marek was determined. Yet how could she stand by and let such a thing happen?

"I know what you plan to do now. I could go to the authorities and have you stopped."

"You could, but you won't. Besides, you wouldn't want that on your conscience—aiding a Nazi who murdered my family, would you?"

"I don't want it on my conscience that I did nothing to stop you murdering a man, either!"

"Then don't look."

"I just can't forget about it, Stefan."

"I don't know why not. Americans have been very good about glossing over what happened thirty years ago to the Jews and the Slavs and Gypsies. Just walk away, like a good little American. This didn't happen to you, so you can't be worried about it."

"That's unfair!" She was stung by his words. She *did* care; she just couldn't condone the killing.

"Yeah, it is." He shrugged, turned around and looked out the window.

She stood for a moment longer, not knowing what to do or to say, and wondering how Stefan felt. He didn't seem to relish the idea of murdering Thorne. Maybe it was hard for him. Yet he was compelled to do it.

And she wondered at the demons that wrestled within this complex man.

The voices were so faint that Astrid couldn't distinguish the words, only the sound, so she tried ignoring them. Only that didn't prove very successful, and now they sounded more like angry bees, and that was irritating her even more. She smelled something awful, something like burned chicken, and that bothered her just as much as the irritating sound.

She waved her hand to make the bees go away, only they didn't. It was so much easier to keep her eyes closed and to just drift away, to pretend that nothing had happened, that she was just floating along on a comforting grayness. She could feel the first faint hammering of a headache, and she could have cried knowing that soon the pain would be racking her. But crying never helped. It would only make things worse.

If only Jessica Mae hadn't been so naughty today. If only she hadn't run away. Astrid squeezed her eyes shut more tightly. She didn't want to think about anything as unpleasant as that, not when she had such a terrible headache coming on. Maybe she would feel better in the morning; maybe she could cope better then—maybe Jessica Mae would be back then, and this nasty episode could be quickly forgotten.

\*　　\*　　\*

[ 173 ]

"Astrid! Astrid, wake up!" Patrick shook his wife reclining on the couch, but she was either sound asleep or had fainted again. Or faking it, he thought with disgust. Astrid had fainted several times since she'd discovered that Jessie had run off. Frankly, she hadn't been much help since the cops had arrived; he'd had to answer all their questions, and what the hell did he know? He had gotten home and the kid was gone. Period.

Jessie. He shook his head. Damned kid. It was turning out that she was more trouble than she was worth. He looked up apologetically at one of the cops. "I'm sorry, I can't wake her up."

The first cop to arrive—Litchfield, his nametag read—was an older guy, maybe in his fifties, with the beginning of a belly. He still looked fairly physically fit, though, Patrick thought, and he had done the most talking. The other cop, Garibaldi, who looked like a rookie, had mostly just nodded.

Right now Litchfield was looking sympathetic. "That's all right, Mr. Fields; you don't need to try to wake her up any more. I've seen this sort of thing happen a lot when mothers—or fathers—are overwrought. We have the information we need right now. Your neighbor gave us a description of what the girl was wearing the last time she saw her. I think we can work with that."

Patrick turned away from Astrid; he was fed up with her theatrics, which left him having to do all the talking; the kid wasn't even his, for God's sake. He'd deal with her when the cops left. "So what will you do now?" He had to ask, after all. Astrid would want to know eventually, when she woke up. And no doubt with a headache.

"We'll alert some of the other units, and have them be on the lookout for her. We'll put out reports for bus stations and train stations throughout the county and state and New York City for someone matching her description. You have to understand we can't call out searchers now. It would take us hours to get something like that organized, and frankly, with it being dark, it would be almost impossible to conduct a good search. Plus we still can't confirm that it's an actual runaway incident yet."

"Yeah, I understand. I told you I think the kid just got pissed at me and her mom, and ran off. I really think she'll be back in the morning. She's probably hiding some place in the neighborhood and laughing at all the trouble she's causing. Or maybe she's over at some friend's house and telling her friend what a pair of dummies we are, you know?"

The two cops exchanged looks, then Litchfield stuck his pad in his shirt pocket.

"Well, thank you, Mr. Fields, for your cooperation. Give us a call if you hear anything tonight—or come up with any leads—and we'll do the same. In the morning, if Jessica still hasn't returned home, we can talk about organizing a search."

"Yeah, maybe she's at a friend's house. We called all her buddies from school—although to tell you, she doesn't have many friends, since we just moved here—and nobody has seen her. Of course, that doesn't mean they're not lying through their teeth. You know how kids are. They can lie with the best of them." He moved to the door. "Thanks, officers. We appreciate your concern."

Litchfield nodded and left the house, followed by Garibaldi.

The two cops paused by Litchfield's patrol car, and watched as Patrick closed the door and then pulled shut the curtains in the front window.

Litchfield shook his head.

"What a bastard," the young cop said. "I'd hate to have him as my stepfather."

"My thoughts precisely," Litchfield said. "You smell the beer on that one?" He shook his head. "She wasn't much better, although I'd bet a week's salary she goes in for stuff like sherry. Much more ladylike." He wasn't sure if her faint—real or otherwise—was caused by the strain or by her drinking. "I'm gonna start looking at the north end of town, Mike. Why don't you go south? I don't think she'd leave town tonight. Where would she go? The stepfather said they're new, so anything outside is going to be pretty unfamiliar. Let's hit some of the spots where kids hang out."

"Sure thing, Joe. Meet you later, though, okay, to check notes?"

"Sure."

"Later." Garibaldi got into his car, waved and drove off.

"Officer."

Litchfield paused in the process of getting into his car and looked up. It was the Wallace woman. A dark-haired man had followed her out of the house. The man hadn't been there before when he'd interviewed her. He glanced over at the dark car in the driveway. "Ma'am?"

She stepped closer so that she could speak without raising her voice. Litchfield got the feeling she didn't want the girl's stepfather to overhear them speaking. He didn't blame her.

"I was wondering what was happening now. Will you be searching for Jessie?"

"Yes, ma'am, my partner and me will be going up and down streets, and I'll alert some of the other officers and have them do the same. Plus we'll be putting out bulletins and such."

"What about search parties?" the dark-haired man asked quietly.

"Well, sir, we really can't do anything until daylight. Frankly, we still don't know if the girl has actually run away from home. She may be over at a friend's house and just wants to make her parents worry. Kids that age do funny things like that. The year my son turned fourteen we couldn't keep him home. He kept running away, but luckily he kept running away to a friend's house. Then it all stopped when he was fifteen, and we never had a problem with him again." The cop shrugged. "Kids."

"Thank you, officer, for your help. I hope you're right and she's just at a friend's house." The woman stepped back as he got in the car.

He thought it was a shame that this woman wasn't the kid's mother. She seemed a lot more concerned than the actual parents.

He backed out of the driveway, and when he glanced back, the couple were still standing there, watching him.

# THIRTY-ONE

"The police are doing nothing until morning? They've got to be kidding!" They hadn't spoken of their heated discussion inside again. They had come to no conclusion, and she suspected they could have argued all night, and they would never see eye to eye. She kept wondering, though, who was right? What if Stefan were wrong? What if Dr. Thorne wasn't this Nazi doctor? What if it were all a case of mistaken identity?

What if it wasn't?

Marek nodded. "It's absurd, but then this is bureaucracy. I can see in one way why they don't rush out with dogs and search teams right away. It would be very expensive to do this for every child who ran away to spend the night at a friend's house."

"This isn't every child," Wendy said softly. "This is Jessie, and I know she wouldn't do that. She's much too thoughtful a child."

"Let's go in and discuss this, okay? I don't like standing in this man's driveway."

*In the open.* She heard the unspoken words, and self-consciously she looked around. But she saw nothing out of the ordinary.

Once inside, Marek stood by the window so that he could gaze out at the street.

"What's out there that fascinates you?" Wendy asked sharply. Her feelings toward him were in turmoil. She was attracted to him, and yet he wanted to murder this man—the man who Marek claimed had killed his family. Perhaps Marek had killed others. Wendy shivered.

"While we were talking in here earlier, I saw a light-colored Mercedes go by several times. Once up the street, twice down."

"It happens, you know. People forget something and have to go to the store, or they go out for a pizza or whatever, or maybe run a

[ 177 ]

kid over to a friend's house. What do we do now? I can't go to bed and sleep, knowing that Jessie might be in trouble. She wouldn't leave home unless she had a good reason."

"Unless . . . ," he said slowly, "unless she was frightened. Remember the other day when she ran into the house, and acted as if someone were chasing her?" Wendy nodded. "What if someone were?" He watched as the light-colored Mercedes drove by again ever so slowly. "Maybe she was being chased. You see that car?"

Wendy glanced out the window. They were in no danger of being spotted, since neither one had yet turned on a light in the room. "Yes." Stefan seemed altogether comfortable in the dark, and that thought unnerved her slightly.

"Dr. Thorne has a silver Mercedes." He looked down at her.

"Oh c'mon, Stefan, you're just being paranoid."

He whirled around and gripped her by the shoulders; the action so startled her she just stared at him. His fingers pressed into her. He gazed down at her intently, and she was aware of how close he stood to her, of his body heat, of the slightly lemony smell of his aftershave.

"I am not being paranoid," he said flatly, "nor imaginative. I would have been dead long ago if I acted in that way. I do not tilt at windmills. I think it is too much of a coincidence—Jessie being chased, Thorne having a silver Mercedes, and now a similar car driving past *her* house—not once, but many times in the course of the last hour. I have been following him around town since I arrived, and I trailed him to the junior high. He drove by it a number of times, and there was no reason for him to be there, believe me."

He relaxed and as he withdrew his hands, he gently brushed a lock of her hair away from where it had fallen over her eyes. Then he stepped away, and for a moment Wendy almost said, *don't.* That was nonsense, she told herself, utter nonsense.

"You don't think that he could have been chasing her that day, do you? She acted so strangely around him, and later when I saw him at the diner, he was very solicitous of her."

His lip curled. "Of course he was. He is a supremely talented actor. Underneath it all he is still a Nazi. And maybe he has learned about Ružena. Perhaps he sees a threat. I just know that where he has been over the past three decades there have been other unexplained deaths, deaths that can only be tied to him."

"Oh my God. But then what's he doing here?"

"He's looking for Jessie," Marek said quietly. He watched as the

Mercedes turned the corner. "I don't think he'll be back. I think he has gone hunting. Just as we must do now. We have to find her first. Get a jacket and some flashlights."

As she got ready, Wendy said, "You know, I don't think Dudley ran off on his own. I think he went with Jessie; either she coaxed him along or he just followed on his own. Why don't we drive around and I'll call Dudley. He might bark and lead us to her."

"It's worth a try. Anything is worth a try at this point."

They hurried out to the Buick. As they got in, Wendy glanced back at her neighbors' house, and saw Patrick Fields standing at the door looking out. She wondered if he would go looking for Jessie, and she decided he wouldn't; he probably couldn't be bothered with such a thing. She shook her head and then they drove off, and all thought of Jessie's stepfather was pushed from her mind.

Where would a young child go at this time of night? Thorne asked himself. A Bach toccata played on the radio and he hummed wordlessly to it; he reached over and turned up the volume. Tonight there had been a program of all-Bach pieces, and it had been quite enjoyable.

Pizza parlor? Too easy. The place would close eventually—no doubt about eleven, if that late—and she would have to go home. It's worth a try, though. She might be there. She might just have decided to leave her family for the night.

He wondered what the stepfather was like. The mother was certainly no prize, and he wondered what had happened to the child's natural father. Divorce or death? He would figure it was probably the former. Mrs. Fields certainly looked the slattern part.

He knew that the girl hadn't returned home. The police had left already, so they must not be organizing a search. He had had many patients who "ran away," only to return to their families within a few hours. Often the child was at a friend's house or even as close as the backyard. Children were a peculiar lot. It was one of the reasons he had chosen to treat them long ago.

He swung by Donnie's Pizza Parlor, parked, and went inside and ordered a slice of pizza. As he waited for it, he glanced around. The place was fairly packed for a Thursday night, and the music—some rock piece by some new band; he didn't pay attention to pop artists—played on the jukebox. The noise was too loud and grating, and there was a sour smell to the room.

Several kids sat in the booths by the jukebox, but none close to

[ 179 ]

her age. Several he recognized as his patients from some years ago, and one or two waved to him. He smiled in response. He paid the counter man and thanked him, then went outside with his pizza slice, which he promptly dumped into the nearest wastebasket.

There was another pizza parlor across town and he drove toward it, keeping an eye on the streets all along. The bus station in Morristown was too far away for her to reach on foot, and the police would be crawling all over it by now. The closest train station was in Boonton miles away, and he doubted she would have hopped aboard a train. Surely she didn't have the presence of mind for that sort of thing. Where would she go?

No, she had stayed in the area. She was new to town, the neighbor had said. She didn't know many people. She wouldn't turn to anyone. He knew that about her.

He checked the second pizza parlor, then went by a fast-food place and checked that out. No one who looked like her. There were a lot of children out on a school night, though, and he frowned at that. His father and mother had always insisted that he go to bed by nine on a school night; weekends he had been able to stay up until ten.

American parents were far too lenient; their children whined at them for the slightest thing, and they gave in without a protest. It was one of the reasons he so despised Americans. He had lived among them for decades, but that didn't mean he loved them.

He drove slowly by the Olympian Diner, but saw no child resembling Jessie. He was fast running out of places to search.

Unless of course she was simply wandering up and down the streets. She could elude searchers for hours that way, no doubt. She was also bound to grow tired after a while; she would have to rest—somewhere.

He drove up and down the streets of Hunters Heights, making sure he wasn't seen by any of the patrol cars he spotted here and there. He didn't want them reporting him for suspicious activity.

At one point he pulled over and ducked below the level of the car window as a police car turned the corner. His windows were down, and he turned down the radio to hear better. Faintly he heard a woman's voice calling a name over and over. It sounded like she was calling a pet. He waited a few minutes, then sat up cautiously. The cop was gone. The woman's voice was closer now, and he watched as a dark car drove past on the cross street.

It was Wendy Wallace, and she was calling "Dudley."

Dudley?

A dog or a cat perhaps.

And the Jew was driving her. Interesting. He hadn't known they knew each other. Very, very interesting.

Now it seemed a pet was missing.

And the girl was missing.

Perhaps, he told himself with a smile, there was a connection. Just perhaps . . .

Maybe he should follow them. They might well lead him to the child.

But first he would go home and change cars. The Jew had seem him too often in the Mercedes, and he didn't like that. His other car, his wife's, was a dark sedan, anonymous. Perfect for the job.

# FRIDAY

# THIRTY-TWO

Thorne had followed the couple discreetly for several hours now and it looked like they knew less than he did. If that was at all possible.

At one point he had pulled into an all-night gas station and had the tank filled, then he had gone back out on the road. The woman and the Jew weren't hard to catch up to; they were driving barely above ten miles an hour. All the while the woman was calling for her pet. Surely she must be getting hoarse by now.

He had switched off the radio long ago. The Bach had gone away, to be replaced by a program of music by Stravinsky and Dvořák. That's when he'd shut the damned thing off. He hated the Slavic composers. They were so inferior in their ability to anything Austria or Germany had ever produced. It had been that way thirty, forty years ago; it was that way now, and always would be. If only people would realize that. Besides, weren't Stravinsky and Dvořák Jews? There was only one thing worse than music by a Slav—music by a Jew. It was the same with literature. So much was made of the writings of Franz Kafka—a Bohemian Jew, for Christ's sake. Thorne shook his head.

He swung back by Clark Street and saw that the lights in the Fieldses' house were all out. Some concerned parents, he snorted to himself.

Then he went driving up and down the streets again. Most people were in bed, now that it was after one in the morning. Here and there some houses still had a few lights on. Most people would be getting up around six or so and heading in to work.

As he should be. But not tomorrow.

This thing had to be resolved tonight.

He yawned. He had no time to be tired now. He must be alert to any clue.

[ 185 ]

Where could the damned child be?

For a change of pace, Thorne headed out of town. He didn't know what he expected to see, but maybe he'd find some clue. Perhaps bread crumbs, such as Hansel and Gretel dropped in the forest.

Thorne smiled at the thought.

Babes in the wood.

The woods!

He glanced at the woods along either side of the road, the woods that surrounded Hunters Heights, and he wondered whether Jessie might have fled there. It was unlikely.

But not impossible.

He stopped at another all-night gas station and bought a map of the county. There were a number of roads that led through the forested areas, roads that were barely wider than a single lane; roads, he suspected, that were better suited for someone on foot or on horseback than someone in a car.

Still, he could try.

He had nothing to lose by doing so.

He chose a narrow road off to the left and cautiously went down it. The moon was out by now, and he dimmed his headlights. He didn't want to signal his arrival, after all. He rolled down his windows on either side so he could hear better. The trees and bushes grew so close to the road that branches scraped the car, and he was glad he had put the Mercedes in the garage for the night.

A moment later he heard something crashing in the underbrush to his right and braked again. Suddenly a doe leaped onto the road in front of him. He was able to stop just in time. The animal stared at him for a moment, then leaped away, followed by several others. Apparently the stag had already crossed the road just seconds before Thorne arrived.

Hunting season would be opening soon, he knew, and the deer, sensing it, were already on the move. He had noted that with each autumn they seemed to flee back into the more inaccessible regions.

He just hoped the little girl hadn't.

He continued along the road until he reached a crossroad, which he traveled down for several miles. It was dark here, with no houses anywhere near, no sign of people. He saw another deer, this one not so fortunate in its crossing. The carcass sprawled to one side. Something had been at it already, and half its flank was missing.

Wild animals, or possibly town dogs that sometimes ran in packs through the woods.

Thorne peered into the darkness. He saw nothing but an owl swooping down once, almost crashing into his windshield, and he had jerked back before realizing the animal couldn't get him.

He listened intently, but heard nothing but the soughing of the wind and the scraping of branches above him, and the occasional cry of a night bird. It was cooler now, and he wished he could drive with the windows up; but if he did that, he might miss something crucial. He decided he must suffer the chill; to compensate he turned on the heater.

He glanced at the clock on the dashboard. 2:13.

He rubbed a hand over his face. He was incredibly weary; this hours-long search had taken its toll on him; he didn't remember being this tired in a long time. After all he was not, as he had to remind himself, a young man any more. He had patients tomorrow morning after his rounds at the hospital. He had a very busy day on this last working day before the awards ceremony. He should go home and get to bed.

He couldn't let this rest. He would be unable to sleep if he didn't find the girl.

He chose another road, and then still another that crossed it, and yet another lane. He'd had no idea that the woods were criss-crossed with these roads; but then there was much about Hunters Heights that he didn't know.

Finally, it was two-thirty. How many more hours could he keep this up? How long? He yawned, and told himself he had to keep going. He had no choice.

He hadn't seen another car in hours; doubtless everyone in the area was asleep—except him. His staff would give him hell tomorrow when he came in. Mrs. Peterson would be especially bad, saying he wasn't taking good care of himself. Which was true enough tonight.

He finished with one road and started on another, not far from the gas station where he'd purchased the map. He drove slowly along it, again seeing nothing, hearing nothing. He wondered if he weren't so tired that he might miss something. Perhaps he should simply turn around and go home and try to get some sleep; then he could start searching in the afternoon.

No, this matter had to be settled. Tonight. If possible.

He realized finally that his bladder was full. He stopped the car, got outside, and urinated against a tree, listening to the sounds of the splashing. He hummed under his breath.

Finally, he zipped up his pants and was about to get back into the car—he had decided any more searching tonight . . . this morning . . . was useless, and he would go home—when something in the distance, deep in the woods and far from the road, caught his attention.

He squinted and could just make it out. Something flickering. Like a fire.

It could be the fire of some bum, he told himself, as he tried to quell the sudden pounding of his heart. It could be something completely different.

It could be, but he knew it wasn't.

He heard a faint noise, cocked his head, and listened. He could hear a dog barking.

In the darkness he smiled.

# THIRTY-THREE

"It's after two-thirty," Marek said. "What do you want to do, Wendy?"

She tried hard not to yawn. She rubbed her eyes and looked out the side window. "I want to keep looking for her as long as possible, Stefan. I keep thinking it's just a matter of time."

She took a sip from the cup of soda she held. Some time ago they had stopped at the convenience store around the corner from her house and had purchased large sodas with lots of ice and a couple of sandwiches. She didn't remember when she had last eaten, and while the sandwiches had not been bad, she really hadn't enjoyed the tuna. It all tasted like cardboard. Now her throat was getting hoarse from all the calling. When she had taken a break, Marek had taken over calling for Dudley.

They had both decided it was best to continue to do so. Maybe if the dog heard his name, he would bark, and they would hear it. They had heard lots of barking dogs—most of whom they'd probably awakened, she thought ruefully—but nothing that Wendy recognized as Dudley's distinct sound. She didn't want to call out Jessie's name. What if Thorne heard? She shuddered. She hated the thought that he was out here . . . there . . . wherever . . . looking for Jessie, just as they were.

What if he found her first?

What if he had already found her?

No, she wouldn't allow herself to think such a thing. They would find her first.

Period.

For quite some time Stefan and she had talked while they drove through the streets of Hunters Heights. She had asked him what he would do . . . afterward . . . and he had replied that he would return to his country. She had felt a little sad at that thought, but knew he had no other choice. Finally, the talking had trailed away, and the only sound in the car had been her calling Dudley's name.

She was aware of an increasing pressure in her bladder. "Would you mind stopping there?" Wendy asked. "I've got to use the facilities."

"No problem."

Marek eased the car into the gas station along the highway, and Wendy got out and asked the sleepy-looking attendant for the key. He handed her one on with a chunk of wood attached to it. Nobody was going to lose that anytime soon, she thought wryly.

She went around to the side and unlocked the door, and flipped on the light. A large black bug scuttled across the floor, and she wrinkled her nose. It crawled into a crack in the wall, and she glanced around, wondering if any of its buddies were here. Nothing that she could see, except that thing in the corner by the toilet.

She bent to get a better glimpse. It was a class ring, a man's. She picked it up and turned it around and around in her fingers.

Jessie wore a man's class ring, a reminder of her father.

She clutched the ring and left the bathroom. She went into the office and returned the key to the man and asked, "Did a girl come by here sometime around dusk or so? A blond girl with a black cocker spaniel?"

The guy covered a yawn and scratched his head. "Yeah, I saw her, and the dog. I had just come onto my shift—well, actually I'm covering a shift and a half, one of our guys is out sick. Yeah, the girl now, she bought a map and a candy bar as I recall."

Wendy forced herself to speak calmly. She couldn't yell at this man or grab him by the shoulders and shake him, although she felt like it. She tried to smile casually, although she felt anything but casual. "Did you happen to see where she went?"

"As a matter of fact, I did. She sat down over there"—he pointed toward a fallen log by the road—"and then headed into the woods."

Wendy's heart sank. "The woods?"

"Yeah, well, really the old road there that goes through the woods. I thought it was kind of odd a kid being out at that hour, but she seemed to know where she was going, and I thought she might live in that new development down the road. I see those kids walking up and down here pretty often, going into town, I guess."

Wendy nodded, not really listening. "Do you think you could point the road out to me?"

"Sure thing."

He walked out of the gas station, Wendy following. She beckoned to Marek, who got out of the car. When they reached the log, the attendant pointed ahead.

"There's a road that goes down there. It's not very wide. More for horses, if you know what I mean. They used it in the old days when the mines were in full operation, but I don't think anyone much uses it these days, unless you count the hikers."

"Thank you, Glen," she said, reading the name patch on his uniform. "You've been very helpful."

"Is the kid in trouble?" he asked, looking a little worried.

"No. Not now. She ran away, and we're trying to get her home."

They headed back to the car, and Marek paused as he was about to get by and looked at the attendant.

"By the way, you didn't happen to see a silver Mercedes go by anytime this evening, did you?"

Glen scratched his head. "Nope, can't say that I did. Saw an oil truck, and a school bus, which looked like it had hit the wrong road. And a couple of other cars, but no Mercedes. I would have remembered that. Not many cars come along here. It's not the best place for a gas station," he admitted ruefully.

"We'll be back tomorrow to fill up," Marek promised as they got into the car. They waved to Glen, who returned the gesture and went back to the office to finish reading the magazine he'd been looking at when Wendy approached him. "Now where's that road? Ah, here we go."

He turned down the path, and involuntarily ducked as a low-hanging branch scraped the top of the car. God, this rental was going to have to be rehauled from stem to stern by the time he returned it. If he did. If he lived. If, if, if.

"I'm turning off the lights," he said quietly. "Just in case."

Wendy nodded. "I'll roll down my window." It was better, she knew, to make a quiet approach, one where they couldn't be seen. If anyone was out here.

They went barely five miles an hour. She couldn't speak; she didn't know what to say. She still gripped the class ring and could feel its edge cutting into her palm. She ignored the pain.

They were close to Jessie, she just knew it.

Down the road over two miles away from the highway they spotted a car pulled over to one side, half on the road, half on what passed as a shoulder. Marek instantly braked the Buick and killed the engine. They couldn't tell what make it was, just that it wasn't a Mercedes.

"We'll get out here," he said quietly, and she heard a tone in his voice that she had never heard before. It sent a chill down her back.

Wendy started to reach for the door handle, and he touched her arm.

"No. Wait." He reached up and unfastened the overhead bulb. "Now you can open the door, but don't close the door; it might make noise that carries."

He climbed out his side, then went around and helped her out. A slight ditch ran along her side, and they both stumbled a bit when she finally got out.

He headed for the other car, Wendy following. She heard a quiet snick and knew he had taken out the gun and cocked the hammer. It was the first time she knew that he had been carrying it all along. He must, she supposed, be ready at all times.

She carried both flashlights in her purse.

The car wasn't a Mercedes, but a dark sedan. The windows on both sides were open, and Marek checked around the car, but could find no one. He opened the glove compartment and retrieved the registration. Wendy took out a flashlight and shone it on the paper.

The name Thorne leaped out at them.

Marek murmured, "I do not think he is out here for his nightly constitutional. I just pray that we're not too late."

He closed the compartment and had just turned away when they both heard it: a dog barking.

"Dudley!" Wendy cried. Dudley was out there, and with him she would find Jessie. Jessie was nearby, and the girl needed her. That much she knew.

She started running.

# THIRTY-FOUR

Jessie woke suddenly, and for a moment she was disoriented. She blinked as she remembered where she was. She had fallen asleep on the floor of the mine, her head resting on her jacket. The fire was dying down, but she still felt its warmth on her face. Too bad she didn't bring marshmallows, she thought, yawning.

And Dudley was barking.

That was what had awakened her, she realized.

"Dudley, hush."

The dog continued to bark. He stood at the front of the mine and barked into the darkness. He could probably be heard for miles and miles, she thought with dismay.

"Dudley, quiet! Come here!" she commanded. He looked at her, wavered. "Come here!" She said it in her fiercest, most adult voice.

The dog growled once into the darkness, then hung his head and padded over to her.

"You're a bad boy, Dud, very bad." He licked her hand dolefully. "I don't think you can make it up to me that way now."

His tail lifted slightly and wagged hesitantly.

"No, you're still a bad boy."

The tail drooped.

She sighed. It was hard to stay mad at him. She stroked his silky ears, and he licked her hand, his tail beating a furious tattoo.

She decided she ought to toss some more wood onto the fire. She got up and stretched. She threw a branch onto the fire, and watched as sparks shot upward. She rummaged through her knapsack. Time for a snack. She gave Dudley a dog biscuit, which he ate in one gulp.

"You're supposed to eat it slowly to savor the flavor," she said, then giggled aloud as she thought how silly that sounded.

Dudley barked.

She put a finger to her lips. "Sssshh!" She took out an apple and began eating.

Was her mother staying up all night, pacing the floors and sobbing about the loss of her only child, while Patrick went out looking for her? No. She figured her mother had gotten a doozy of a headache, and Patrick was swigging down beers and getting louder and coarser, and her mother would have fled to the quiet darkness of her bedroom, and Patrick would sit on the couch downstairs and watch TV and drink beer and fall asleep.

Would they think of her? she wondered. Her mother would, Jessie told herself. She really would.

Tomorrow when it was light and she could see, she'd make her way home. She would face the music. She knew she would be punished. Patrick would probably hit her. Her mother would cry if he did, but that wouldn't stop him. Then he would make her take a shower.

Jessie shuddered.

She finished the apple and tossed the core into the fire, and listened as it sizzled. For a moment she could smell the apple fragrance, then it was gone.

To be replaced by a stench she knew all too well. Slowly around her things turned gray.

"No," she moaned aloud, forcing herself to stay alert.

A twig snapped outside the mine's entrance, and Jessie's head jerked up.

Suddenly she knew just how vulnerable she was. The fire lit up the mine entrance, pinpointing her. She felt cold, and she reached for her knapsack and carefully drew out the knife she'd put there earlier. Then she started inching back toward the niche, pulling the knapsack and Dudley with her.

The dog bared his teeth and began growling.

She was too late.

"Good evening, Jessica," Dr. Thorne said formally, and the light from the fire glinted on the weapon in his hand as he stood in the entrance.

Jessie said nothing. She swallowed heavily. She had been caught.

"So, it looks like you've run away for nothing," Thorne said, moving toward her. The .38 trained on her never wavered, nor did his unblinking gaze.

Jessie's lower lip wobbled, and she bit down hard, drawing blood. She didn't care; she wouldn't show him that she was afraid.

Dudley continued to growl, then barked once, then again quickly.

"Hush," she said. Inside she was very cold, and the voices that she had heard so often seemed too close.

"Very wise, young lady. If your dog doesn't behave, I shall be force to shoot it!"

"No!" She grabbed Dudley to her chest and hugged him tightly. "Let him go." In her other hand she still held the knife, concealed by her pants leg.

Thorne simply smiled. He blinked once.

"I want to know how you knew."

She frowned. "Knew what?" She could feel the faintness coming on again, and she knew that if she had a spell now, she would die. This man would see to it.

"Don't be coy with me."

"I don't understand."

"You are a most wearisome child, Jessica," he said, shaking his head. "I want to know how you knew who I was. That's all."

"My neighbor took me to see you. That's how I learned your name."

"You idiot child!"

Jessie blinked at the sound in his voice. The grayness wanted to envelop her, and with each breath she fought it.

"I mean the other name. You called me by it that day I met you in the woods."

She didn't know what he was talking about; she wasn't sure that he knew. She suspected she'd better humor him, but she didn't know how. So she didn't say anything. She didn't know how to answer.

"Speak up, child." He leveled the pistol at her.

Dudley barked suddenly, his nose twitching as he looked toward the mine entrance, and started wiggling his stumpy tail.

"I haven't all night, you know. So, tell me, how did you know my old name? Come, come, it doesn't matter what you say, child. You're going to die in the end anyway."

"No!" screamed Wendy as she launched herself from behind Thorne. She managed to hit the doctor squarely in the back, making him stumble and loosen his grip on the pistol, which fell to the ground. Effortlessly Thorne shrugged Wendy off and backhanded her, and she staggered backward.

"No!" Jessie ran forward and stabbed at his leg with the knife.

Thorne screamed, hit her with one hand, and lunged for the automatic, just as Marek showed up. Thorne whirled and fired at the other man, hitting him in the arm. The 9 mm flew backward into the bushes outside the mine.

"So, things are not quite as you thought they would be," Thorne said with his gun pointed at Jessie, his voice calm. His breathing wasn't labored; it was as if he hadn't exerted himself. Carefully he stooped to pick up the knife so that Jessie couldn't get it. Jessie stood there, not knowing what to do.

As Wendy got to her feet, she saw Marek's bleeding arm and gasped. Marek just stared at the doctor.

"Tell me, what are *you* doing here, Jew?" Thorne asked, his tone almost humorous. "Why is everyone gathered here tonight?"

"I've followed you a long time, Dr. Dornmann. A clever name, 'Thorne.' 'Dorn,'" he said to Wendy, his eyes never leaving the other man's face, "means 'thorn.'" He paused. "Your long flight is over, though. I've come to kill you."

Thorne arched an eyebrow. "Have you now? Why would you want to do such a deed? And how is it that you think you know me?"

"I first saw you in Auschwitz, where you sent my family to their deaths."

"But not you. What a pity." Thorne chuckled, and Wendy felt the hair rise on the nape of her neck. "So yet another Jew has come in a feeble attempt to kill me. And failed, as I had no doubt you would, as all the others have through the years. It's no wonder really that you all walked into the ovens, like the brainless sheep you are. You died in the millions because of your stupidity, because you never had the guts of a real man to fight back."

Marek stared at Thorne, then walked evenly toward him, his arm hanging by his side. Blood dripped onto the ground.

Thorne chuckled again and fired when the other man was only a few yards away, and Marek went down.

"No!" Wendy raced to the fallen man. She could see the wound the bullet had made in his right side, but his chest was rising and falling. He was alive. His eyes were open and he was gazing straight at her. He mouthed a word. "Run."

"And now, my dears, to finish you off," Thorne said in his most suave voice. "I must get home soon. I have work in the morning, and then as you know, the following evening I'm receiving my humanitarian award."

Wendy picked up the flashlight she'd dropped, then rose slowly to her feet and flung the handful of dirt she'd gathered by Marek's side. It hit the doctor straight in the eyes, and the shot he got off hit the mine's wall. He clawed at his eyes.

"Run, Wendy!" Marek screamed. "Get away!"

"This way!" Jessie pointed toward the right-hand tunnel.

Wendy grabbed Jessie's hand and they raced down the black tunnel, past the pool of water, with the dog running close behind. Suddenly she heard something pinging off the stone wall beyond her head.

Thorne was following them and shooting. It was only a matter of time, Wendy realized with dismay, before he got lucky and hit one of them.

She could have cried in her frustration.

There had to be a way to get away from this madman, she told herself. Somehow.

If only she knew.

# THIRTY-FIVE

Gradually Wendy slowed their pace. She feared the doctor might catch up with them, but she didn't want to run into something she couldn't get out of—a sunken shaft or a pit. In the darkness she couldn't tell. She had to depend on her sixth sense at this point, and a whole lot of luck. She stretched out one hand to touch the tunnel wall; that way she'd know when they reached a cross-tunnel. And then what?

Their only chance of survival depended on her finding a way out of the mines.

"Did you go down this tunnel?" she asked Jessie as they raced along.

"No," the girl gasped. "I was scared to. I didn't know what I would find."

Wendy was running Jessie ragged and she wanted to slow down even more, but knew they didn't dare. Thorne would catch up to them then, and he had a weapon. They didn't have anything.

The floor of the tunnel began sloping downward, and Wendy almost stumbled. She realized they were getting farther below ground. She didn't want that; she wanted to find some way out to the surface. But maybe, she reasoned, they'd have to go down first to go up.

She had no idea where the tunnel led—perhaps it was a dead end, perhaps it led to a lower level that would simply trap them—but she had to take a chance on following it; she certainly couldn't return the way they'd come. Some of the mines, she knew from the articles she'd read in the newspaper over the years, had multiple entrances, and she was praying this was no exception.

They came to a place where the air current felt different, and she suspected that they had reached a branch in the tunnel; her hand hadn't encountered space, so she supposed the branch jutted off to the left. The sounds of pursuit had grown fainter.

She risked flicking on the flashlight quickly, took a few steps forward, and realized that her toes were hanging over a void. She stumbled back hastily, nearly knocking Jessie down.

"There's a hole there. I don't know how far it goes down, and we can't risk trying to jump across it," she whispered to Jessie.

"Then we have to go to the left," the girl said, her voice equally low.

Wendy nodded, although Jessie couldn't see the gesture, and gripping her hand tighter, she turned to the left-hand tunnel. This extension angled downward too, but they continued along it. They had no choice.

Maybe they would be lucky, and the doctor would pitch head-first into that hole. He didn't have a flashlight like they did.

Or maybe he would simply stand still and listen to the sounds of their progress.

"We must be as quiet as possible," Wendy whispered, her lips close to the girl's ear.

Wendy could hear Jessie breathing harshly, and she wondered if the little girl was going to have a spell. Not here, not now, she prayed, and squeezed Jessie's hand. Jessie squeezed back.

Now they slowed to a walk—there was rubble underfoot and Wendy didn't want to risk either one falling and getting hurt—and after some time she felt cool air against her face and turned in that direction. She paused and listened, but could hear nothing behind them.

Some of the mine shafts were located under the town and under various housing developments. She wondered if they were running for their lives under someone's basement or root cellar, and it almost made her smile.

That expression quickly faded as she wondered about Marek. Had Thorne left him alone? She had heard only the one shot fired at them. That didn't mean he'd left Marek alive, though.

She couldn't think about it, could only think about getting out of here, getting away from Thorne—getting Jessie away from him.

Jessie clung tightly to Wendy. The girl hadn't spoken in a while—but what, Wendy asked herself, was there to say?

Her face felt gritty from the dust they had raised and which clung now to her skin, and her lips were so dry. She licked them, and took a long ragged breath.

[ 199 ]

Silence, and then the sound of a shoe hitting a pebble, which rattled along. Jessie gasped, and Wendy pulled her closer. Somehow Thorne was managing to keep up. He was physically fit and healthy, but they were so much younger; surely they could outlast him; he was bound to become winded before they did. Suddenly he fired a second time, and then a third time. Again he missed with both shots. Blind shots, blind luck. She just hoped luck continued to be on their side.

Six shots altogether. Maybe he would run out of ammunition. Maybe he had spare clips with him, she thought fearfully.

There was a deep grumbling within the mine, and Wendy ran even faster. The rumbling increased, and she dove into a side tunnel, just as a mountain of rock and boards cascaded down behind them.

The floor and sides of the mine shook with the cave-in, as she cradled Jessie tightly against her, shielding her face. Finally, the thundering subsided, and only the dust whirled around them. She coughed and so did Jessie.

"Dudley?" Jessie asked, wheezing.

Wendy took out a flashlight and flicked it on. Dudley whimpered. He was only a few feet away, and a small rock had hit him in the side, but otherwise he was okay. He wobbled over, and Jessie hugged him tightly.

For a moment Wendy could do nothing. She had to sit and catch her breath and think ahead. She wondered if the cave-in had stopped Thorne. He might well be pinned under the rock and dirt.

Then again, he might not.

She stood, even though she had a cramp in her side. She couldn't give in to such things now. She had to think about Jessie—and Dudley, she added, looking at the girl huddled with the dog.

"Jessie," she whispered, "we have to go now."

"Yes."

Wendy frowned. The answer was so formal for the girl. She looked into Jessie's eyes, and knew then that she was looking at Ruzena. The girl smiled, and Wendy smiled back.

"We must go."

She helped the girl to her feet and turned off the flashlight. Dudley limped after them. She could hear his panting. Her heart was pounding, and the stitch in her side had increased.

Jessie cried out, and Wendy turned the flashlight on her. A piece of long-discarded metal lay near a tunnel wall, and Jessie had run into it. Her jeans were torn, and Wendy saw blood trickling down her leg. The girl would need a tetanus shot when they got out of here. If they did, she reminded herself.

"Okay?" she asked.

The girl nodded.

A few minutes later Wendy felt fresh air moving against her face, and she knew there must be another entrance up ahead.

She took a deep breath and forced herself to think rationally, and kept moving as she found the floor slanting gradually upward again. The air grew cooler and she knew she was close.

She could see stars up at an angle, and there was enough light from the moon outside that she saw she would have scramble up a slope. This must be where the miners from long ago had dumped waste rock that had been removed from the shafts they'd sunk into the mine, or perhaps this slope was used to move heavy equipment into the mine. For whatever reason, it was damned steep. This would take some doing for them both.

"We have to go up this slope," she whispered, her lips close to the girl's ear, "and we must do it quickly."

The girl nodded.

"Here goes," Wendy told herself, and with a deep breath she started to heave the girl up the slope. Then she started to follow. Dudley was already scampering upward, his claws clicking on the rocks.

Suddenly Jessie slipped on a pebble and lost her footing. She slid down the slope, knocking Wendy back as well.

There was a chuckle from behind them, and in that moment Wendy knew that Thorne had not been caught by the cave-in after all, but had indeed somehow circled around through the various tunnels and met up with them.

There was no escaping now.

# THIRTY-SIX

In the moonlight Wendy saw Thorne standing not far from them. He raised his pistol and struck Wendy, and she cried out. Her hand went to her cheek and she felt the blood. She could hear Thorne's ragged breathing. Dudley was barking, the sounds echoing against the stone walls, and Thorne whirled around, raising the pistol to shoot the dog standing at the crest of the slope.

Without hesitating, Wendy grabbed the flashlight and brought it down against the back of Thorne's head. He sagged slightly, and she started toward Jessie, who was staring at the man.

Thorne raised the automatic toward her now. "Are you a Jewess? I think so. You and the man are well-suited, you know. You Jews never could finish a job." He chuckled at his own humor.

Wendy gazed at him in surprise. The blow had only momentarily stunned him—she thought she had hit him with all her strength. Apparently not. Before she could do anything, he raised his arm and hit her again, and she fell back against the mine wall.

He flung himself on her, and she fought, amazed at the older man's strength. She struggled against him and managed to flip him over. Blindly she reached out, but could find nothing. Then suddenly Jessie was standing above them and in her hand she held a fair-sized rock. She raised it, then realized what she was about to do.

She paused.

Thorne laughed.

Wendy could hear all the years of scorn and hatred in this man's voice, and she thought of what Stefan had suffered in Auschwitz, and she thought of his lost family, of all the lost families, and all the little lost girls like Ruzena who had come back across the years seeking someone to find her killer.

Wendy grabbed the flashlight again and with all her strength struck Thorne alongside the face with it just as Jessie slammed the rock down on top of his head. Wendy heard a sickening wet sound, and Jessie, who was sobbing now, brought the rock down again and again. Jessie would have bludgeoned the man more, but Wendy leapt up to grab the girl's hand, and the bloody rock tumbled from her other hand. Then Wendy scrambled up the slope.

She didn't look back; she couldn't risk it. Dudley raced in front of her, barking and barking, and she feared she would stumble over him.

Suddenly there was a crack of a pistol, and something hot stung her side and arm, and she realized with shock that she'd been shot. He still wasn't dead; he wasn't even disabled. Tears of frustration blurred her eyes.

She thrust Jessie in front of her, trying to protect her.

"*Raus!*" the girl shouted. "*Raus!*"

There was another shot, this one just missing them. It hit a branch to one side, and the wood snapped.

And suddenly behind them came a massive rumbling, and Thorne fired again.

The reverberation increased, and as Wendy glanced back, she saw that Thorne was trying to crawl out of the mine, but it was too late.

The crumbling timbers and unsteady rock crashed downward, pinning him. He screamed and cried out for help, but Wendy and Jessie kept running.

Thorne's shrieks grew fainter, and now Wendy could see Stefan's rental car far to her left, and up ahead was Thorne's car. All that running around underground had mostly been in circles; they hadn't gone all that far away from the main entrance to the mine. She clasped Jessie closer and stumbled to the entrance.

Stefan had managed to crawl closer to the fire to keep warm, and Wendy dropped to her knees by him.

"Are you all right?" she asked, gazing at his bruised face. He had torn off part of his shirt and stopped the bleeding in his arm, but she could see that the wound in his side was still oozing.

"Fine, just fine," he said, his voice barely above a whisper.

She brushed the hair from his forehead. She knew he was hardly that. None of them were in peak condition at the moment, and she almost smiled at the image. All of them—even the dog—had been injured. In a fight for their lives, she thought soberly. The pressing need to do something had passed, and for the first time since she

[ 203 ]

had thrown herself at Thorne she could sit and rest. She was bone-weary.

Jessie just sat, gazing at Stefan.

"What about her?" he asked.

Wendy shook her head. "She scraped her leg in the tunnel, but I think she's okay otherwise."

Dudley had disappeared into the niche and returned dragging the knapsack toward them.

"What's this?" Wendy asked him, and opened the knapsack and peered in. "Well, well, Jessie packed pretty well when she decided to run away. Soda?" she asked, bringing one out. Stefan nodded, and she popped the top and held the can to his lips.

Now, that she was no longer running, she grew aware of the burning pain in her side. She touched her side and her fingers came away red; she wiped them on her jeans.

"Thorne?" Stefan asked, after he had swallowed a few mouthfuls of liquid. Wendy handed a soda to the little girl, who took it unseeingly.

"Pinned in a cave-in by one of the entrances. We got out just in time."

"Dead or alive?"

"I don't know. I didn't check. I guess I should."

"No!" He clutched her hand. "It might be a trap for you. We should get out of here."

Wendy looked around. "Are your keys still in the car?" He nodded, then winced. "Okay, look, I'll be back. I don't want either of you walking far, okay?" Again he nodded.

She headed back to the car and as she did so she glanced at the other mine entrance. She could hear rocks still sliding down. She could hear no other movement, though.

She started the Buick and edged into the woods, picking her way around trees, driving over bushes, and hitting a few potholes and boulders; she would be lucky if she didn't tear off one of the axles. She hoped Stefan's insurance would pay for all this damage.

She braked, then hit the high beams and studied the cave-in. She saw Thorne, his upper torso on this side of the rock slide, his head propped against a large boulder as it were his pillow. His face was white, almost pinched looking, and blood dribbled down the rocks into the soil. One arm was trapped, the other stuck straight out—the arm with the .38, which had dropped from his fingers. He was not moving. She honked the car horn; he didn't twitch. She should get out and check just to make sure, she knew, but she feared what she would find. She had never seen a dead man before. She had written about death all the time in her books, but never seen it in real life, and tonight she didn't want details.

Finally she worked the car as close to the mine entrance as she could, and ordered Dudley into the car. He leaped in and barked.

"Peppy, isn't he?" she said as she helped Stefan to his feet. He grimaced but made no sound, and she eased him into the back seat.

Then she went back to get Jessie, who had curled up by the fire. She picked up the girl's knapsack and slung it over one shoulder, and then discovered she'd lost her purse in her flight somewhere. She shrugged. She would find it tomorrow or the next day. It wasn't all that important, after all.

Wendy put the girl into the car on the passenger side and closed the door. Jessie opened her eyes and sleepily murmured *"je tomu konec,"* and Wendy didn't need a translator to know that meant "it's over." Jessie would be all right.

She kicked out the fire, then started the car and slowly made her way back to the road. As she passed the station, she glanced at it, but it was dark. Glen had gone home finally, and well he might, she thought as she glanced with shock at the dashboard clock.

It was nearly five.

She yawned and headed toward Hunters Heights Hospital. Boy, were those emergency-room people in for a surprise tonight.

This morning, she corrected herself, as she looked down at Jessie sleeping on the seat, the dog curled up in her arms.

Finally, those ghosts—Jessie's and Stefan's—had been laid to rest.

And while she was certainly sorry he had been injured, Wendy realized he wouldn't be going home right away. She smiled. That would give them time to get their story right. She figured the cops would be very interested in what had gone on out here tonight.

She yawned again, and felt a contentedness go through her.

Shalom, she whispered aloud. *Peace.* For them all.

And she smiled in the darkness.